THE GARDEN

CAROL MATAS

THE GARDEN

cover art by
Janet Wilson

Scholastic Canada Ltd.
Toronto, New York, London, Sydney, Auckland

Canadian Cataloguing in Publication Data
Matas. Carol, 1949-
The garden
Sequel to After the war.
ISBN 0-590-12381-5
1. Holocaust survivors - Juvenile fiction. 2. Kibbutzim-
Juvenile fiction. 3. Israel - History - Juvenile fiction.
I. Title.
PS8576.A7994G37 1997   jC318í.54   C97-930461-X
PZ7.M423964Ga 1997

Published simultaneously in the United States
by Simon and Schuster Books for Young Readers
Book design by Anahid Hamparian.
Cover design by Yüksel Hassan.

5 4 3 2 1   Printed and bound in USA   7 8 9 /9

For my mother, Ruth,
a true warrior,
with love

ACKNOWLEDGMENTS

I WOULD LIKE TO THANK THE MANY PEOPLE WHO HAVE HELPED ME IN MY RESEARCH AND IN THE WRITING OF THIS BOOK.

FIRST THOSE WHO HELPED ME IN MY RESEARCH: PNINA ZILBERMAN, DIRECTOR OF THE HOLOCAUST EDUCATION AND MEMORIAL CENTRE OF TORONTO, WHO ORGANIZED MANY OF MY INTERVIEWS WITH SURVIVORS; AND THE WONDERFUL PEOPLE WHO WERE SO BRAVE AND GENEROUS IN RELIVING THEIR EXPERIENCES FOR ME: YAEL SPIER COHEN, HENRY MELNICK, VICTOR GUTH, YEHUDAH SINGER, NECHEMIA WURMAN, LEONARD SHERMAN, PINCHUS LEVINE, SIMON SLIVKA, SHMUEL SEGEV, JOE LERER, SAM SINGER.

AND THOSE WHO HELPED ME IN THE ACTUAL WRITING OF THE BOOK: MY EDITOR, DAVID GALE, FOR HIS ATTENTION TO ALL DETAILS OF THE BOOK AND HIS THOUGHTFUL EDITING; HIS ASSISTANT, MICHAEL CONATHAN, FOR HIS ALWAYS CHEERFUL WILLINGNESS TO HELP; PERRY NODELMAN FOR HIS INSIGHTFUL CRITIQUES—I MADE HIM READ IT MORE THAN ONCE!; MY HUSBAND, PER BRASK, WHO LISTENED FAITHFULLY TO THE BOOK, CHAPTER BY CHAPTER; DIANE KERNER AT SCHOLASTIC CANADA FOR HER SUPPORT AND BELIEF IN THE BOOK; NINA THOMPSON AT THE WINNIPEG JEWISH PUBLIC LIBRARY FOR HER HELP AND HER INDULGENCE FOR MY VERY OVERDUE BOOKS; PNINA ZILBERMAN, WHO READ THE MANUSCRIPT FOR ACCURACY AND HELPED WITH THE GLOSSARY; PATTI COHEN FOR RECOMMENDING BOAZ RAFAELI, AN ISRAELI LIVING IN WINNIPEG, WHO KINDLY ANSWERED MY INQUIRIES ABOUT SNAKES, FLOWERS, CROPS, AND GUNS; MICHAEL NEWMAN FOR HIS HELP WITH THE INITIAL RESEARCH; DONNA BABCOCK FOR TYPING THE

MANUSCRIPT; AND TIM BABCOCK FOR RUNNING AN UNOFFICIAL COURIER SERVICE. AND JANEEN KOBRINSKY, WHO WAS EXTREMELY GOOD-NATURED WHEN I INTERRUPTED HER PAINTING TO REQUEST THE WORDS FOR HORAS AND LULLABIES.

A GRACE

this end is come
the time to bind our teachings

to our hearts and give thanks
for the steely souls seeking

refuge in the shadow by the rock
of life with its hollows and openings

inviting them to slip through the unimagined
and unwrap a new heritage a crown for the age

—PER BRASK

NOVEMBER—DECEMBER 1947

CHAPTER 1

The viper stares at me, its triangular head, covered in brown and orange spots, swaying a little from side to side. I am frozen.

"Use your spade," Assiya hisses.

I realize that I am clutching a spade in my hand. Slowly, I begin to raise it, but the snake notices, turning slightly toward the motion of my arm. I'm sure it is ready to strike. I leap away from the viper, at the same time bringing the spade down on its head. It attacks just when I do. Still, I manage to smash the side of its head. It twitches, then lies dead in the dirt.

I turn to Assiya with a weak smile. She grins back at me. "Good," she says, her Hebrew limited, my Arabic just about nonexistent. She takes her shovel and throws the snake away.

Assiya likes coming to work in the garden while her mother is at Morris's clinic with Assiya's little brother, who is often sick. Assiya has become a sort of unofficial assistant to me and I enjoy her company. Her family lives in the Arab village, Majed, which is perched on a hill overlooking Kibbutz David.

In the summer, the snakes are everywhere. They should be slowing down now, as the weather cools. But the last week or so has been unusually warm, so the snakes are more active than I'd like. Morris has promised me a cat to help control them. I make a mental note to remind him again.

I've spent the morning planting, getting the garden ready for the rainy season. Because of the warm climate I always have some flowers in bloom. Even though it's November and I have cut down most of my perennials, my roses are looking perfect, as are the bougainvillea. The kibbutzniks wander in and out all the time, just to look and smell, and relax.

I'm proud of my job here as the kibbutz gardener. When I arrived in Eretz Israel over a year ago, after a long difficult journey from Poland, I was in bad shape. Almost all my family had died, murdered by the Nazis. The doctor here, Morris, decided that I needed to work in the flower garden, that it would be therapeutic.

There was a lot of therapy in the children's camp where I stayed in Italy, and even at the detention camp in Cyprus. But that involved talking. I liked Morris's idea much better. He didn't make me talk, he let me work alone; he let me have a little peace.

At first, Pnina taught me gardening. Then she was needed in the kitchen, so they put me in charge of the garden and all the flower beds around the kibbutz. It's my job to make this place as beautiful as possible. It makes me so happy to take care of the flowers and the cactuses, to watch them grow and bloom. And happiness is a feeling I was sure I'd never have again.

"Ruth! Ruth!"

The garden has been planted in a plot of land right beside the main building, just off the central square. Nathan is standing on the road which curves like a horseshoe in front of the main building. He is waving something white in the air as he calls me. I make a shrugging gesture to Assiya. She leaves to find her mother at the clinic. I run over to Nate.

"What is it? What's that?"

"This," he answers, "is your nurse's uniform. I've managed to get an ambulance on loan from a hospital in Tel Aviv but I've promised to have it back by tonight. Run and change now. I'll fill you in on the rest later."

A horn beeps just behind me and I jump a little, involuntarily. I turn to see Zvi sitting behind the wheel of the ambulance, grinning.

I shake my head at him, grab the uniform from Nate, and start to go over to the main house, to change.

"Wait," Nate calls.

He runs after me and gives me a bag. In it are shoes, stockings, and a hat. Once in the main house I find an empty classroom where I change quickly. I have an awful time trying to fit my long black hair under the cap—in the last year it has grown and become wild and curly. Finally I twist it so tightly it hurts my scalp, but it stays in place. I emerge, I imagine, looking every bit the professional nurse.

Nate and Zvi are waiting for me, dressed in British Army uniforms, Nate's with a captain's epaulets. Zvi twirls his walking stick.

"Well?" He grins.

"Very handsome," I say. And although I instinctively hate uniforms, it does seem to suit Zvi. Of course, it doesn't hurt that he is almost six feet tall, with skin brown as a nut from the sun, black hair that is thick and wavy, and large eyes almost as dark as his hair. I'd hardly recognize him as that scrawny boy I met on the train as we escaped Poland over a year ago. But he still wears his round glasses, and he always has a joke for me. Or a kiss.

Nate has been the leader of our group since he led us out of Poland to Eretz Israel. Sometimes to tease him we call him Moses. He's managed to keep us older ones together, bringing all of us to this kibbutz. Now he's head of our Palmach section. Sometimes that makes him a little unpopular—like when he forces us to run five miles with fifty-pound packs on our backs. And if we complain we always get the same answer. "You asked to be in the Palmach. We are supposed to be the crack troops of the Haganah, and that means training, training, and more training."

He's not much taller than me—I'm only five feet four inches—and he's thin all over. Thin nose, thin mouth, small wiry body, but a look of compassion in his eyes, like he cares about you—and he does. He's in his twenties. Practically old around here.

"Is anyone going to tell me what we're about to do?" I ask.

"We are going to drive that ambulance," says Nate, "into a British Army camp, pay fifty pounds to a young sergeant who's looking for quick cash, and drive away with thirty guns. Let's go."

The three of us scramble into the cab of the ambulance.

Our kibbutz is situated just off the Tel Aviv–Jerusalem road, about thirty minutes by car from Tel Aviv. Nate tells us that the army barracks we are going to are on the outskirts of Tel Aviv. He puts the siren on for the entire trip so we won't be stopped by British troops. I try not to think about what might happen if we are caught buying guns in a British Army camp. Straight to jail, that's certain. Possibly a death sentence. I worry less for myself than for Nate and Zvi. The British are apparently quite soft on the women they encounter, but they have no such scruples with the men.

"One day Mr. Abrams visits a doctor." Zvi has obviously decided to distract me. He seems to know when I worry or am upset almost before I do.

"The doctor looks him over and pronounces him healthy.

"'But I have a terrible headache!' objects Mr. Abrams.

"'Oh,' says the doctor, 'that doesn't worry me.'

"'Well, doctor,' says Mr. Abrams, 'if you had my headache, I wouldn't worry about it either.'"

Nate laughs. "I've heard that another way," he says. "Two men in a congregation are talking. 'Our cantor is superb,' says one. 'So what,' says the other. 'If I had his voice, I'd sing just as well.'"

"I'm telling doctor jokes," Zvi scolds Nathan. "Don't get sidetracked." He pauses.

"Okay. Little Moshe says to little Sarah, 'A chicken just came by and told me what kind of a man your father is.'"

"'What kind?' asks Sarah.

"'Cheep, cheep,' laughs Moshe.

"'Well,' Sarah replies, 'guess what? A little duck just came by and told me what kind of doctor your father is!'"

"Look lively," Nate mutters, cutting Zvi off, "here we are, faster than I thought. Act British!"

"Yes sir!" Zvi says.

"Right ho!" I snap out sharply, two words from my limited English vocabulary. I can understand it pretty well now, but speaking it is another matter entirely.

"Good lad," says Nate in English. "And lady," he adds.

That makes me giggle.

"No giggling. British nurses *never* giggle."

"No sir!" I say in my best imitation accent.

We drive up to the guard post, sirens wailing, and the guards wave us through. Nate drives the ambulance down the outside road of the camp, as directed, and stops when he sees a sergeant motioning to him. We all leap out, Zvi and I opening the back doors.

Nate hands over the money. The sergeant nods, counts it, then nods at us. We begin to load the guns into the ambulance.

"Bloody hell."

The sergeant swears under his breath, and stares down the road. A jeep is driving straight toward us. For a second we are all paralyzed. Then Nate hisses, "Be a nurse." He and Zvi grab a sheet from the cot in the ambulance. They throw it over the guns. Then Nate tosses me a stethoscope from the first aid box in back. I point to the sheet, motioning the sergeant to sit on the guns. He does so, obviously too terrified to think for himself.

I place the stethoscope over his heart. The sound almost deafens me. His heart is hammering so loud I'm afraid he might have a real heart attack.

The jeep slows down. It looks like there are two enlisted men driving in it.

Nate motions them on. They see that he is an officer. One of them speaks. "Everything all right, sir? Need any help? An escort?"

"No, private," says Nate. "Carry on. False alarm. Too many figs."

The sergeant motions them away as well.

"Thanks, lads," he says, his voice shaky. "Worst case of heartburn I've ever had. Thought the old ticker was giving out."

I smile sweetly.

The privates grin and one says, "If she'll come look after me, I might just eat a crate of figs. Look at those big blue eyes!"

I pretend to be embarrassed and I look down at my toes. The soldiers laugh, and then they drive off.

The sergeant is pouring sweat. It drops onto the stethoscope. I pull it away, hurry around him, fling open the doors of the ambulance, and pull the sheet off the guns. Nate and Zvi start throwing the guns in. I join in, and so does the sergeant. Finally they are all loaded. I slam the doors as Nate leaps into the driver's seat. Zvi and I climb in the back and we peel away, sirens blaring. I'm pretty sure my heart would sound the same as the British sergeant's if anyone were to listen. We get to the camp gates and Nate calls to us, "They're going to check us! Zvi, there are guns under the cot."

Zvi reaches down and comes up with two handguns. He gives one to me. I put it under the mattress.

Frantically we shove the rifles under the sheet as far away from the door as we can. Zvi rips off his jacket and lies down on the cot. He holds his gun just under his back so he can pull it out quickly and use it if he has to. I wrap the blood pressure band around his arm and lean over him with the stethoscope.

Nate screeches to a halt.

"Heart attack!" he yells. "Let us through."

Out of the corner of my eye I see soldiers peer in the back window. I slip one hand under the mattress and wrap it around the gun. For a moment nothing happens. Zvi and I stop breathing. Then the guard raps on the back door with his fist.

"Good luck!" he calls.

Nate puts his foot on the gas and we careen out of the camp, onto the open road. Nate keeps the siren on.

I stare out the window watching for any pursuit, but to my relief the road is clear, outside of the usual traffic of cars, buses, and the occasional donkey and rider.

The fields are bare now. We have to wait for the first rain before we can plow and seed the winter crops. I remember when I first saw this land at the end of last summer. I expected it to be all desert and cactus. Instead, I found corn and wheat waving in the wind, everything gold and brown, rolling hills covered in pine trees. The air shimmered in the heat. And there were olive trees, older than forever, strange and exotic. I fell in love with it. Maybe because nothing about it reminded me of Poland or of Germany. Instead, it is memories waiting to happen.

We drive through an Arab village, and I can't help but think about what might happen next week, after the United Nations vote on partition. If the vote is for partition, we'll need these guns because many Arabs don't want to split the land, they don't want to share it with us Jews, they just want us to leave. Instead of *us* leaving, though, it'll be the British, and then what? Some kind of civil war between Arab and Jew?

I've only been here a year and a bit but when I first arrived the kibbutzniks and the Arabs from Majed, the village on the hill, were very friendly. Sometimes when there were disputes to be decided that related to the village and the kibbutz, the Arabs would host lavish dinners. The women from the village brought their sick children to Morris's clinic every Wednesday morning, and the Arab children attended school at the kibbutz. But in September the Arab children stopped coming to school, and lately the clinic sees only those children who are *very* sick—like Assiya's little brother.

The leader of the Arabs in Palestine, Haj Amin Husseini, the Grand Mufti of Jerusalem, hates Jews. He was an ally of Hitler's during the war. He's ordering the Arabs to fight, and those who don't want to are finding his men in their villages, ready to *force* them to fight.

Yehudah, as head of the kibbutz, tries to keep us informed. After dinner in the big dining hall, he gives a short talk and lets us know the latest developments. The closer we get to a vote the worse things look, and the more important these few guns become.

When we get back to the kibbutz, Nate drives straight for a small hill, the front of which is covered in twigs and wood. As we approach, six kibbutz members lift up an entire wall made of twigs, leaves, and wood to reveal a tunnel that has been dug out of the hill, large enough for a number of vehicles. I try not to show how amazed I am. Somehow this huge hole was dug without any of us knowing—probably on those days when all of the young people and children were out on two- or three-day hikes. I smile to myself but try to look composed in the faint light of the oil lamps. After all, I *am* a Palmachnik. Nothing should surprise me. Nate drives the ambulance in and the men rush in after, closing the fake front behind them.

"Now we hide the guns." Nate smiles. "And after dark, I'll return the ambulance. We'll split the arms up, no one knowing where they all are. Zvi, you and Ruth take one box.

"Good job," he says. And we scramble out of the ambulance to help unpack the guns.

CHAPTER 2

I am finding it hard to stay awake. Zvi and I were up most of the night, burying the guns. We chose a spot just behind the garden, in an old dirt patch that leads into one of our wheat fields. I have to concentrate, though, because I am doing some grafting work with my roses and if I'm not careful I'll ruin the graft.

Suddenly the kitchen bell begins to ring. I look at the sun. I'd lost track of time, I know that, but it couldn't be dinner already. And now I can hear the sound of jeeps, but I realize that they can't be ours. Our jeeps rattle and clank and backfire. These are running smoothly and there are lots of them.

I race toward the center square in time to see six jeeps full of British soldiers screech to a halt. The soldiers pour out and the sergeant in charge is met by Yehudah.

"What can I do for you?" Yehudah asks.

"Checking for illegal arms," the sergeant replies.

I stay calm on the outside, but inside my stomach twists into a knot.

"It would save us all a lot of bother if you just handed them over. And," he adds, "it'll save your property as well."

Yehudah is a man in his fifties who grew up on this kibbutz. His face is tanned from the sun, his hair is still thick and curly, if a touch gray. He flashes the soldiers a smile and waves them on.

"Please," he says, "be our guests. We have nothing to hide."

My heart is beating so hard in my chest I'm sure if they get close to me they'll arrest me for hiding some secret weapon inside my shirt. I try to appear as casual as the rest. Everyone who isn't working in the fields has come to the square. Zvi catches my eye. I'll bet he came in early to snatch a little nap before dinner.

The soldiers march into the dining hall in the main building. A few of us, including Yehudah, follow them. They begin to rip up the floorboards. We *had* hidden some guns under the dining room floor, but we moved them a couple of months ago. Finding nothing there, they begin to go from building to building, shoving bookshelves over in the schoolrooms, toppling furniture and beds in the residences, all with smooth, ruthless efficiency. Finally they end up in the children's quarters.

So far the soldiers haven't found anything, but I know we're not safe yet. I hate them for crashing into our kibbutz; it reminds me of the way the Nazis would crash into a home to do as they pleased and no one could stop them. All those feelings of helplessness are rising up in me. I want to forget those feelings, I never want to feel that way again! I know in my head that the British aren't the Nazis, but the rest of me can't seem to tell the difference.

I run after the soldiers and follow them into the children's house. Varda has put the children to sleep on their mats on the floor. The sergeant stops, uncertain for a moment. I hold my breath. Then he barks, "Get them up! Right now!"

The children, many of whom were only pretending to sleep, take their time getting off the mats. The little ones in cribs begin to cry. Yehudah tries to stop the soldiers, shouting, "These are children! Have you no feeling? Get out of here!"

He's dragged outside and I follow. A couple of soldiers start to beat him badly. There is a horrible thud as a boot crashes into his head, a crack as another lands on his ribs. They are demanding to know where the guns are. I feel so helpless, unable to fight, unable to stop the ones in the room inside, knowing what they will find.

Soon they come out holding a dozen bren guns up in the air, triumphantly. It must make them mad to see we've somehow smuggled in these machine guns from Czechoslovakia—one soldier leaps into his jeep, another throws the guns on the ground, and their jeep backs over the guns, then moves forward. They make a horrible crunching noise as they are flattened. I see Rivka and Zvi, their eyes watering, biting their lips, refusing to give the British the satisfaction of seeing them cry. I'm too angry for tears. Those pitiful twelve guns could have saved the lives of those very children in there. And what we went through to get them! *And* I know that while the British are taking away our guns, they are *selling* guns to the Arab states—and those guns quickly end up here in Palestine. It makes my blood boil. Still, they haven't found the biggest cache yet. I find myself praying to God that they won't—even though I don't even know if I believe in Him anymore.

They continue to rip up the kibbutz, finally ending up in my garden.

"Not my roses!" I shout. "Look, you can see the ground hasn't been touched. Don't pull up my garden!"

One of the men, a young fellow with red hair, sniffs a rose.

"They're beautiful," he says. He looks at his companion. "I don't think we need to look here, do you?"

His companion shakes his head. But then the sergeant is there, his round red face pouring sweat, his little eyes glinting.

"Dig it all up," he orders. "There aren't only a dozen guns hidden in this kibbutz."

I watch in horror as they pick up the shovels I had left there and begin to plow into the soft dirt. I don't know what comes over me, I'm a trained fighter now, supposedly disciplined, but when I see my roses tossed aside as if they don't matter, I go a little crazy and throw myself at the soldiers, frantically trying to grab the shovels out of their hands. One of them pulls a shovel away from me and swings it, hitting me square between my shoulder blades. All the air goes out of my lungs and I slump to the ground. Zvi, who couldn't move fast enough to stop me, rushes over and pulls me up.

"Ruth," he says, "are you all right?"

I nod. I can't quite catch my breath, though. I turn my head and look at the soldiers digging, flinging dirt and flowers everywhere. A lump of dark earth and broken stems lands at my feet. As my breath returns I start to mumble, "I'm going to kill them, I'm going to *kill* them."

"What's she saying?" one of them asks.

"Nothing," Zvi replies, "she's just upset."

"She'll be a lot more upset if she lands in jail," the other remarks, the one who didn't want to ruin my garden. "Try to keep her quiet."

"Ruth," Zvi whispers in my ear, "we can't do anything. Please be quiet."

At that I turn my head away. I can't watch. Finally they are done. No guns. They throw down the shovels and walk away. I notice that the nice one looks back with what could be a kind of regret. I've heard the English love their gardens at home. Maybe this one made him remember his own, and made him remember peaceful, lovely things so different from the life of a soldier. But he destroyed it anyway.

They arrest Yehudah for the dozen bren guns they found, promising to take him to the hospital first because he has a horrible gash in his head and pain when he breathes. The soldiers probably broke some of his ribs when they worked him over. Tires screeching, they pull out of the square, a trail of dust following them.

I sink to my knees in the dirt of my garden. My back aches where I was hit.

"Ruth," Zvi says, "just tell me what to do. Can we save any of it?"

I look at the devastation all around me.

I shake my head.

Fanny runs up to me. "Ruth, I'm so sorry," she says, but I

can see by the gleam in her eye she's not at all sorry, because they've missed the big stash of guns under the earth only a few yards away.

"We'll have to replace those guns they took," Zvi says. "Right away."

I nod.

"I'll see what I can organize," he says.

I pick up a crushed red rose and stare at it. I almost laugh. Well, God answered my prayer, didn't He? What a sense of humor He must have.

"Never mind," says Fanny, "it's just a *flower*. The guns are what's important here."

"Fanny," Zvi says, "don't be stupid."

Fanny looks at Zvi in surprise, then back at me. She pauses. "I'm sorry, Ruth, I shouldn't have said that."

I shrug. What does it matter? It's what she thinks; what they all think. And my head knows that they're right. But my heart knows something else.

And then, in the fading light, I see my brother Simon walking briskly up the road. I immediately burst into tears and run over to him. He hugs me. I show him my ruined garden.

He shakes his head in disgust. "The pigs," he says. "Never mind, Ruth. One day this whole land will be ours and you can plant flowers across every inch of it, if you want to."

"How did you get here? I'm so glad to see you."

"A friend of mine was driving past here and offered me a ride—I'd been saying I wanted to see you. I'm lucky I just missed the British. Wouldn't they love to capture an Irgun fighter."

"I'm so glad you came." Just seeing Simon makes me feel better.

Simon pats Zvi on the back. "And you, Zvi, how's everything?"

Zvi forces a smile. "Fine, Simon. But has it ever occurred to anyone in *your* headquarters that we wouldn't be suffering these horrible raids, and this"—he gestures at the destruction we're standing in—"if the British weren't so furious over what *you* and your precious Irgun were doing!"

Here we go.

"If it weren't for us, the British would stay here forever," Simon says. "And you know it."

"No I don't," Zvi retorts. "The vote on partition at the UN is in a week. We need world opinion on our side. The Irgun is too extreme—you act like a bunch of terrorists."

Simon looks grim. "If they shoot us, we shoot back. If they hang one of ours, we hang three of theirs. That's it. That's the way it'll be. I'll never back down from another fight."

I kick at the dirt. "If I have to listen to you two go on and on, I'll probably have to kill both of you," I declare.

They look at me sheepishly.

"I'm sorry, Ruth," says Zvi.

"Me too," says Simon. "You must be heartbroken."

"Well, I am," I say to Simon. "Even though I know perfectly well no one else really cares about my flowers. Because at least the guns weren't found."

"Of course everyone cares," Zvi objects. "It's just that with the vote in a week . . ."

"I know," I sigh. "With the vote in a week, we could need the guns right away. We can't shoot with flowers, can we?"

My voice must sound bitter enough that it shuts them both up.

And now I have to wonder if Simon is so wrong after all. I've always agreed with the peaceful approach, the defensive approach of the Haganah. And look where it got me. Maybe if Simon and his Irgun friends had been here, they could have stopped the British from doing this. When we arrived in Palestine I couldn't believe Simon joined the Irgun instead of the Haganah. Suddenly I understand his decision a whole lot better.

Rivka arrives then, and so do Karl, Sima, Nate, and

Miriam. Ever since we made that trip from Poland over a year ago, this group has stuck together.

Sima begins to sing. It's a beautiful song, with a sweet, haunting melody. The sun has set now, the moon and stars shine down on us. The others join in. And slowly I do, too. At least we are still together. But I look at my garden and wonder if we will end up like that in the weeks and months to come—broken, crushed. After all, there are millions of Arabs and so few of us. If they decide to fight, how could we survive?

CHAPTER 3

I am sitting on a bus, bound for Jerusalem. When Simon and I first found each other, after the war, he shocked me, telling me that our aunt Sophie and her daughter, Mika, had also survived the war, and that they were living in Palestine. Aunt Sophie often sends me messages and arranges for me to come and visit her in Jerusalem.

It's been a week since the British raided our kibbutz. We've had one light rain, so I've been out in the fields with the others, plowing and planting. When Aunt Sophie called last night and invited me to come visit her I jumped at the chance. It's not that I hate working in the fields—it's just that I miss working in my garden.

Aunt Sophie lives in a small house on the outskirts of Jerusalem. The house is nestled into a hill, which is covered with fig trees.

When I arrive she hustles me into the kitchen and immediately begins to feed me. On the kibbutz we are given a very strict diet but she somehow manages to bake sweets of all sorts, so I sit down to tea and coffee cake and strudel.

I look at Aunt Sophie as she bustles around the kitchen. She's just a tiny person—I used to think of her as meek and quiet. I remember Uncle Zev, my father's brother, was loud and always laughing, so that none of us children had ever really noticed Aunt Sophie. Uncle Zev was a doctor and he'd somehow managed to get papers for Aunt Sophie and Mika to get them out of Germany. He was to follow a month later with their two boys, Benjamin and Adam, but they didn't make it. You can see the results of having lost her husband and children and parents—well, her entire family really—in her eyes. She always has dark circles under them, as if she never sleeps.

Mika is married and has a baby, Hani-el, which means "Have mercy on us, God." She's named after Hannah, Aunt Sophie's mother. Aunt Sophie dotes on Hani-el. It's hard to believe when you see her as a loving grandmother just how tough she can be—she has a very high position in the Haganah, although I'm not sure what it is. I think she helped to keep our group from Poland together.

"I wanted you here," she says, "because the vote at the UN is tonight. With the time difference we won't know the results until very late, and I think the family should be together for such an event."

I'm just glad to be here, even though I'm still a little shy around her. But by *family* she means Mika's family and me— Simon is not welcome as long as he's with the Irgun. "They're nothing but a bunch of terrorists," she would say over and over. "Ruining all our good work."

"But he's your nephew!" I'd object.

"Yes, all the more reason for him to behave!" she'd declare and that would be the end of that discussion.

Still, Simon tells me that he does see her occasionally and that she even uses him to pass on messages to the high command of the Irgun. And that he always leaves her house with a piece of strudel in his pocket. There are so few of us left alive in our family. Even though she hates what Simon does, she can't bring herself to cut him off completely. I'm glad of that, at least.

The vote had been planned for the day before but the Israeli delegation had somehow gotten it delayed, playing for time and extra votes. Now finally, it will all be decided. Mika and her husband, Jonathan, come over with the baby, and the house begins to fill up with people. We listen to the radio as one by one each country votes. The Soviet Union votes yes to partition, and so does the United States. Everyone cheers. Now we know a state is possible. Our own country. Never again could a Hitler decide to massacre millions. Never again would we have nowhere in the world to go. If we'd had a state ten years ago I'd still have my family. If. If. No more ifs. I'm tempted to pray again. But why would I? Six million prayers already went unanswered. But maybe—just in case?

My heart is in my throat. I am barely breathing. The tension in the room is terrible. What will we do, where will we go, if they vote against partition? What will happen to those Jews still waiting in Displaced Persons Camps in Europe? Will they have to try to resettle beside the houses stolen from them, the mass graves of their families?

Country after country votes. Yes. Yes. No. Abstention. No. Abstention. Yes. And then finally, Aunt Sophie, who's been adding them all up, looks at us and says, "We have enough. A two-thirds vote. We have it! We've won."

We all stare at her. For a moment the room is completely silent. Then, inside the room and echoing through Jewish Jerusalem, a cry of joy erupts. Mika throws her arms around her mother—and for a moment I am so jealous of them, mother and daughter, I forget about why they are so happy. Then Mika leaps up, takes both me and Jonathan by the hand, and pulls us outside. The others in the room follow. We form a circle under the stars, and we sing, and we dance the hora.

David Melech Israel
Chai chai vikoyom
David Melech Israel
Chai chai vikoyom. . . .

We sing faster and faster and dance faster and faster. And it goes on all night long.

When Aunt Sophie wakes me, it is light. I must have fallen asleep at some point, curled up in a corner of the living room. Aunt Sophie is obviously upset.

"The Arabs in old Jerusalem are rioting," she says. "They're burning shops, looting, stabbing the storekeepers, and the British are standing by doing nothing."

I am wide awake immediately.

"Do you have weapons?" I ask.

"We have a special Haganah unit trying to disperse them," she says, "but the British are stopping our unit from taking action. Still, one section slipped past the British and have pushed the Arabs back to the Jaffa Road. Only now the mob has taken a different direction and is looting in the commercial center instead. The reports are coming in so fast I can barely keep up."

I look at her. If she doesn't want me to fight, what does she want?

"We're afraid the Jews of the city will get so angry with the British for standing by and letting this happen that they'll take matters into their own hands."

Now I'm getting confused. "Isn't that a good thing?"

"No. We don't want this fire to spread to the rest of the country. We will defend ourselves from Arab attacks, of course, but we will *not* initiate attacks on them. Maybe, that way, we can avoid a war. They'll understand that we want to live in peace with them."

I immediately think of Simon. If one Jew is killed, then he and his Irgun fighters will be there to fight back. And it sounds like more than one has been killed.

"Not everyone is going to agree with your policy," I say.

She shrugs. "We know that. But we have to try."

"And?" I am still not sure what I'm supposed to do.

"And we are gathering a group of Haganah who will stop any retaliation against the Arabs by the Jews."

"Stop them! How are we supposed to stop them? Do you want me to fight Jews?" I say, horrified, thinking Simon could be one of them.

"No. Don't fight them. Stop *them* from fighting the Arabs."

Aunt Sophie is tough, sending her own niece on such a mission—but who else can she trust?

She echoes my thought. "I wouldn't ask you," she says, holding my hand, "but we need people right away. We need people we can trust, with some training and some discipline."

I nod reluctantly. I don't like the idea of fighting fellow Jews; in fact, the very thought makes me feel sick. We have *real* enemies to fight, and a little voice inside me wonders if I shouldn't go join Simon. Still, I'm *not* a member of Irgun, I'm a Palmachnik, and I'll go where Aunt Sophie sends me—even if I don't want to. I know her intentions are noble—I just don't *feel* noble.

"No weapons," Aunt Sophie says. "All I can offer is whatever you can find outside."

I splash a little water on my face, then hurry out to the fig trees to see if I can find a stout branch. I pick up a curved one about two feet long and strip it of its twigs, then trot back to the house. There are already about fifteen people waiting, more coming every minute. I notice Mika's husband, Jonathan, among them. He waves me over to him.

"Keep near me, Ruth," he says. "Your aunt Sophie will kill me if anything happens to you."

"Are you in charge?"

"I guess I am," he says, looking around the room. "Quite an army." He turns to the others. "Let's go, people."

On the way out he shows me his truncheon. "Compared to your stick I guess I'm well armed."

I notice that the sun is far up in the sky. I must have slept a good part of the day away. Our little group makes its way into the heart of the city, and what we see there is terrible. The remains of shops smolder, people wail and cry, the hurt and wounded are everywhere. British troops just stand by and watch. We place ourselves on Jaffa Road, the Arabs just behind us. We can hear a mob approaching.

"Turn your back to the Arabs," Jonathan orders.

We do. It's scary. Really scary. I see a crowd of Jews heading straight for us, and just behind us are the Arabs.

The mob gets closer and closer. They see that it is their fellow Jews blocking their way. They can't believe it!

"Move away!"

"Traitors!"

"Who are you protecting?"

"Let us by."

"Join with us!" And on and on.

Jonathan holds firm. He calls out. "We're not budging. We are trying to contain this fight, not spread it! Your actions will only make things worse!"

A young woman steps forward.

"My father is in the hospital, stabbed," she screams. "Our shop is burned to the ground. Get out of our way!"

And she runs forward, almost straight into me. I drop my stick and wrestle with her, finally pushing her back. But the fight has begun. Everyone rushes at us at once and for a few minutes there's the nasty sound of blows being exchanged. I pick up my stick and begin to swing it around. Others brandish their weapons as well. That seems to discourage many in the mob who have no weapons at all. Finally they begin to back away.

"Go home," Jonathan orders. "The Haganah is fighting where we can, but the British are stopping us. We don't need an all-out riot here."

The young woman calls, "We've *had* a riot! And now we need to teach them a lesson!"

"Go home!" Jonathan repeats. "Fighting will only lead to more fighting!"

I have to admit that he is impressive. I'd never really thought much about him. He's not special looking in any way but he has an authority and sincerity which obviously is powerful, because slowly the crowd begins to thin. Naturally a few stay to argue and some of our group can't resist arguing back. But Jonathan doesn't want us with our backs to the Arabs any longer than necessary, so as soon as he feels the danger has passed he moves us out, and gets us back to Aunt Sophie's house.

I'm relieved. It looks like Aunt Sophie's plan has worked and without anyone getting badly hurt. Jonathan was so calm—and I can see now that the Haganah approach makes a lot of sense.

As soon as we arrive Aunt Sophie takes me aside. "You'll have to head back to the kibbutz right away," she says. "If the Arabs are going to fight, the roads won't be safe much longer. I'm going to have Jonathan put you on a bus."

She hugs me. "Take care of yourself, Ruthie," she says.

"I'll try," I say. "But I hope I don't have to go fight any more Jews."

"I hope so, too," she sighs. And she sends me on my way.

CHAPTER 4

I sit on the bus, wondering what will happen now—anxious to get back to the kibbutz and to my Palmach unit. I'm sitting beside a young woman in her twenties. We start to chat. My Hebrew is very good now, with only a slight accent, and I'm happy I've discovered that I have such a good ear. She's a Sabra born in Palestine—in Jerusalem, in fact. The old city of Jerusalem has just been cut off from the new city of Jerusalem by the Arabs, and she can't get home, so she's on her way to relatives in Tel Aviv. She's wearing a long skirt and has her hair covered—she's obviously Orthodox.

"God means us to have this land," she says fervently, "so I know He'll help us." I don't roll my eyes or anything but I'm tempted. I've heard this a hundred times from Simon. "Still," she continues, "I can't believe the change in the Arabs, overnight almost. Our family has shopped in the Arab market all our lives. We were all friends. . . ."

And then—it happens so fast I can hardly take it in—there is a loud crack and the glass behind her shatters and she is still looking at me, eyes wide open, mouth open as if to say something else, but instead she slumps over and I see a big red hole in her back, blood pouring out.

"Down!" I scream. "Everyone get down! Someone's been hit!"

The bus is full and everyone throws themselves on the floor, the driver picking up speed, going as fast as he can. A minute later another shot breaks a window but this time no one is hit.

An older man manages to crawl over to where the girl is slumped on the seat. "Let me look at her," he says. "I'm a doctor."

I've seen so much death in the camps, in the ghetto, I know what it looks like. He checks her, then shakes his head. I think of her poor family, believing that she's safely out of Jerusalem. She was so sure about what God wanted. Would that have extended to her and to her fate? Did God want her dead, too? I can't believe that, any more than I can believe He wants us to live in this land. *We* want to live here. We have roots here five thousand years old. More importantly, we have nowhere else to go. For me, that's enough.

I haven't seen someone die since the summer I traveled here to Palestine over a year ago. I'd tried to blot out those memories—lose them in the fragrance of my flowers. Now they're all threatening to come back. And I have to accept that this is probably just the beginning. But how can I accept it? And what if *I'm* the one called on to kill, to *be* the killer. I find I'm shivering and I can't stop.

The bus shakes and rattles as it moves through Bab el Wad. There are Arab villages all along the road from Jerusalem to Tel Aviv, but especially here, close to Jerusalem. The Arabs can take potshots easily at anyone on the road. How simple it would be to make this road impassable, I think, and to cut Jerusalem off from the rest of the country. After what feels like forever, we finally get out of the deep ravine, hills on either side of us, and then we feel a little bit safer.

Thankfully, no more shots are fired and the rest of the trip, if uncomfortable, is uneventful. When I get back to the kibbutz in the early afternoon, everyone is still celebrating. Lunch finished, they are dancing the hora in the central square. Zvi is so happy to see me, you'd think I'd been gone weeks. In fact, everyone has a hug and a kiss for me.

"A country!" Zvi says, holding my hands in his. "I told you, Ruth. I told you it would happen."

"We're not a country yet," I remind him.

"But the day the British leave, that'll be the day we'll be a country. Until then—it's like an engagement with the marriage to come shortly."

He leans over and kisses me softly on the lips. For a moment I rest my head on his chest, hear his heart pounding, feel his warmth. For a moment, I'm completely happy.

Then Fanny pulls me out of his arms into the hora. "Come on, Ruth, dance! Tomorrow we fight."

I don't ask her if she's serious or not. I'll find out soon enough. For now, I'll dance. I don't want to even think about what just happened on the bus.

We sing, "*Ushavtam mayim b'sasson mimainay hayeshvah.* With joy we shall draw water," a real song of the desert.

Finally I get thirsty from the dance, maybe even from the words. As I'm drinking a long swig of cool water, Nate finds me.

"Oh! Ruth. I have a job for you tomorrow."

My heart sinks. Is this it? The beginning?

"Jerusalem is going to need guns. They have almost none. And you know the only people who the British won't search."

"Girls," I answer.

"Correct," Nate says. "They are true gentlemen. The guns will arrive from Tel Aviv tonight. You'll get on a bus to Jerusalem with the guns hidden in your skirt."

"The girl sitting beside me on the bus was killed on the way here," I say quietly.

"I heard. They're going to try to cover the buses with steel, but the ones tomorrow will just be your ordinary variety. There'll be a convoy though; all the buses will travel together."

"Aren't the British going to even *try* to keep order?" I say. "In Jerusalem they did nothing—they let this horrible riot happen, people killed, shops burned. They just *watched.*"

"My sources tell me that all they want is out of Palestine—as safely as possible."

"But why do we have to smuggle the guns now? They aren't

going to enforce that law? They have to let us have guns now!"

"They don't *have* to do anything. In fact," Nate says, "they arrested people today on gun charges just to make that perfectly clear." He gets up. "See you bright and early."

"Who else is going?"

"There'll be six buses with one Palmachnik per bus. You, Sima, Fanny, and Rivka will each be on a bus. Karl and Zvi will be on the other two."

"Dressed as girls?" I grin.

"No." He smiles. "Although . . . no. Just in case we need to fight and you need some help."

I suddenly feel very tired—no surprise since I probably didn't sleep more than an hour last night—and I slip away to my tent. Fanny is still dancing, so it's quiet and I scramble into my small cot. I find my mind wandering. And then I'm in my garden, but I'm in a deep hole, like a grave, and British soldiers are throwing dirt over me. The hole is filling up quickly and the soil begins to cover my face. I can't breathe, my mouth is full of thick, dark soil, and then it covers my nose and then my eyes. . . . I wake up with a start. A dream. I was dreaming. I look around me. It's dark. I must have slept right through supper and into the night, because Fanny is asleep on a mat on the ground beside me.

Fanny never has bad dreams. Now I'm afraid to go back to sleep. But eventually I must drift off because I wake up suddenly—Fanny is tickling my feet.

I pull them back and snap at her. "I hate it when you do that!"

"Put on your nicest, fullest skirt," says Fanny. "Nate just dropped off the guns." She holds up the various pieces, as they've already been taken apart.

"I only *have* one skirt," I mutter.

"I know that." She grins. "Look, they figure I can hide *three* guns."

Fanny is big. That's the only way to describe her—she's big

everywhere. She could probably hide a submachine gun down her front and no one would notice.

We get dressed and help each other tuck the parts into our clothes and undergarments. Then we walk out of the tent, looking very stiff and silly.

Rivka and Sima are also looking rather uncomfortable.

We waddle over to where the buses are waiting. Zvi, Karl, and Nate are already there.

Zvi has to practically lift me onto the bus, as I can't bend enough to climb the stairs. The buses are already filled with travelers going from Tel Aviv to Jerusalem. Many on my bus look worried, but probably have to make the trip for one reason or another. I certainly would rather be working in my garden.

My breath catches in my throat. For a moment, I'd forgotten that my garden is dead—just like when Mother was killed I would wake up expecting her to be there, until I remembered. . . .

The bus lurches forward and I hang on. I'll have to make the trip standing up. That's obvious.

The road is bumpy and I'm wondering if I shouldn't have at least gone to the bathroom before a ride like this. Wondering? I *know* I should have. And then my stomach starts to growl and I realize that I'm hungry. And of course I can't help but worry that we are sitting ducks for any sniper.

The bus screeches to a stop. British soldiers have just pulled up in front of us.

The windows are open so that in case bullets do hit at least we won't also have to deal with flying glass. But even with them open, it's so hot in here that I'm sweating and the tube-shaped gun part that is stuck into the waistband of my skirt starts to slip. I am just about to put it back in place when a British officer marches onto the bus. I freeze.

He's very tall, maybe six foot four. He checks under the seats in front first, then has a look at the men in the first row.

The part is slipping fast. I put my hand on my waist and try to hold it up. Then another British soldier gets on the bus. This one is young—really young, with freckles all over his nose— and he has his jacket off because of the unusual November heat. He begins to make his way down the bus. At around the halfway point he looks around casually and orders everyone to put their hands in the air so he can check quicker.

If I don't put my hands up, he'll notice. If I do, the slim piece of metal will slip. Maybe. Maybe if I hold my breath and push out my stomach it'll stay put. Gingerly I raise my arms. And slowly, slowly, I can feel it slipping, and—oh, God—it drops right onto the floor.

The young soldier looks sharply my way and then back toward the officer. He moves over to me and drops his jacket.

"Oh," he says, "butterfingers."

I've stopped breathing. My thoughts are racing. I'm wondering what prison will be like, if they've caught Fanny, if Zvi is behaving or if he's thrown himself at them—or if when he sees them take me away, he'll throw himself at them then.

Slowly the young soldier bends over, picks up his jacket.

"Drop your hands," he barks at everyone.

Quickly we all do.

As my hand drops he slips the small metal piece into it.

"All fine here, sir," he calls.

"Right," says the officer. "Let's check the others."

And before I know it, they're both gone.

I let out the breath I've been holding in one mighty sigh of relief.

The crowd on the bus stays silent, waiting. Minutes later, Zvi leaps on and races over to me.

"Everything all right?" he says.

"I'll tell you later," I whisper, "but I had a close call. What about the others?"

"Fanny lay on the floor and we pretended she had typhus.

So they didn't even get on that bus. And they wouldn't search Rivka or Sima even though I think the tall one was suspicious." He squeezes my hand and feels the metal there. His eyebrows raise, and his eyes widen.

"Like I said, close call."

He shakes his head, and hurries off the bus. We start up almost immediately and suddenly I feel quite shaky. As we head into Bab el Wad I begin to feel very nervous. And then the bus jerks to a stop.

"There's some kind of roadblock ahead," the bus driver calls. "Looks like an old car."

I don't have to tell the people here what that means—almost immediately everyone is on the floor. I slide down myself feet first and lie on my back in the aisle. I know Zvi and Karl will be out there moving the car, perfect targets for any sniper. And then I hear the shots. And more shots. I feel helpless. Finally, the bus starts to move.

None of us gets up because as we move the shooting continues.

A bullet ricochets off the wall just over our heads. A woman screams. I try to think of something to occupy my mind. Silently, I repeat all the curses I've learned in Hebrew since I got here. *La'Azazel, Yimach shimha, Tipach Ruhaha, She'TizTaleh B'esh Haghehynom.* Those are my favorites. I say them over and over, especially *Sh'TzTzalech Ba'esh Hah'gehenom,* "You should *fry* in hell." Then, at last, the bus slows and the driver calls out, "We're here. Anyone hit?"

Everyone gets up and, stepping over and around me they hurry off the bus. Do they think I'm lying here for my health? They couldn't have taken one second to stop and help me up? Perhaps they assumed I *could* get up on my own, but I can't. I can't move. I lie here until I see Zvi standing over me.

I'm so happy to see him I can't speak. I kept picturing him hit, wounded, maybe even dead.

"I could just leave you there," he says, a twinkle in his eye.

I realize he wouldn't be teasing me if anyone had been badly hurt. Then I realize what he's threatening. "You wouldn't!"

"I would of course. Unless . . . well, maybe you could convince me."

I try to move but the metal parts are holding me stiff. I'll never get up without help.

"Convince you how, you, you . . ." I think of throwing all the curses I've been practicing at him, but I decide against it. Instead, I try to remember the ones my mother used to use. I speak in Yiddish because only then can you get the real flavor.

"Uh," I say, thinking hard, "may all your teeth fall out except one! And in that one may you get a toothache!"

Zvi smiles. "If you think that is going to convince me, you might want to think again."

"May you grow like an onion—with your head in the ground."

Now Fanny is standing beside Zvi. She's grinning too. "Can't get up, Ruth?"

"May God answer all your prayers—and then may He mistake your worst enemy for you!"

"Oh, Ruthie," Zvi says. "That's not nice!"

"Ruth," scowls Fanny, "I'm ashamed of you!"

"Let me up!" I yell in Hebrew.

"But you look so sweet like that," says Zvi. "So . . . so . . . *helpless.*"

I can't think of any more curses. Then I remember one that Baba used. I just change it a little for the present circumstances. "May you fall into an outhouse just after a regiment of British soldiers finishes a dinner of prune stew and twelve barrels of beer!"

"Okay, that's it," Zvi says. "I don't have to take this. I'm leaving." He turns.

"Zvi, I'll kill you when I get up. I mean it."

"Take guard duty for me tomorrow," he says, "and you'll have a helping hand."

"Fanny!" I plead. "Don't let him get away with this!"

"You're right," she says. "Men!" And she scoops me off the floor in both her arms and lands me on my feet. I realize that she couldn't have bent over that way unless she'd gotten rid of all the metal in her, so I immediately pull all of the gun parts out of my clothing and drop them on the seat beside me.

"Zvi," I glower at him, "you are in BIG trouble."

Zvi backs off the bus, feigning fear. I pick up all the gun parts. "Honestly," I say, shaking my head, "how long would he have left me there?"

"Probably until you agreed to extra guard duty." Fanny laughs. "Never mind."

"Was anyone hurt?" I ask.

"Karl got a nick in the leg. He's being treated in the hospital. Otherwise, everyone seems all right. A miracle really. I'm not looking forward to the ride back."

"Me either." I sigh as we leave the bus. "We might not be so lucky next time." And then I go search for a bathroom.

CHAPTER 5

The return trip to Kibbutz David is nerve-racking since we have no guns. A British convoy watches us most of the way, yet I know they will stand by and do nothing if the Arabs fire on us. Just as I finish thinking this, shots ring out all around us. Zvi and I are sitting together near the front of the bus, the others are near the back. We drop onto the floor.

"If it wasn't for Simon and his Irgun friends attacking and killing the British," Zvi says, "maybe they wouldn't hate us so much. Maybe they'd even help us."

"Zvi, you're such an innocent sometimes," I reply.

A bullet hits the edge of the window just above us. Zvi takes my hand. I hold on to his tightly. We keep talking, just so we don't have to think that we could be dead in the next second.

"The Irgun didn't hurt any of the British in Italy," I say, trying to keep the fear out of my voice, "but the British still did everything they could to stop us from coming here. Who attacked us on the boat, who killed Saul, who stuck us behind barbed wire in Cyprus?"

"I'm not saying I like them," Zvi retorts. "Just that there are some who are fair. You haven't forgotten that fellow who helped you, have you?" he says.

"No, of course I haven't. But there are so few like him."

Actually, inside I'm torn. I hate the Irgun for the violence and carnage they cause but sometimes part of me loves them for fighting back with everything they've got. I love the Haganah for their high principles but sometimes part of me hates them for their high principles, their desire always to do the right thing. Right now, huddled in this bus, helpless, all I want to do is let loose on anyone who might try to hurt me or the people I love.

The shooting stops about five minutes after it starts—it must have been coming from only one village.

When we are finally let off at our kibbutz, we find it unusually quiet. We stand in the square for a moment wondering where everyone is when a shot whistles past my ear. Then another hits the dirt in front of Karl.

"Damn," Zvi exclaims. "Run!"

We race into the main dining room to find about a dozen people huddled in the center of the room.

"They started shooting from Majed an hour ago," Miriam explains as Zvi and I drop to the floor beside her.

"I can't believe they're shooting at us," she says. "It's awful."

"Are the children safe?" I ask. I think of how I had to hide from my enemies at their age, how I don't want that for them. And I start to get angry.

"In the shelters," she replies. "We're to go there when we get the chance."

"Where's Nate?" Zvi wants to know. We all look around. "I thought he'd run in here with us."

"He must be having a little talk with Haganah headquarters," Miriam says. "I saw him head for the communications room. We can't just sit here and let them take potshots at the kibbutz. Plus, Moira was hit and we have to get her to the hospital."

We wait there with the others until Nate shows up. He pulls Zvi and me over. "We need the weapons you buried. Wait until it's dark, then go dig them up. At first light we go into Majed."

My stomach turns over. I've never been in any real action before.

"We take out *only* the houses that have been shooting at

us. Our orders from headquarters are very strict. We are *not* at war. We don't go in against the entire village."

"How will we know who's attacking us?"

"I'm going to find out," he says.

"You'll be shot."

"They won't see me."

"Why should you risk your life that way?" Rivka pipes up. She's been huddled near us the entire time. "We should just go in and take the village. They'll always be a threat to us now." Rivka, although not in the Irgun, believes as Simon does—if they shoot at us, that should be their first and last chance to hurt us.

"Each kibbutz is going to have to decide whether to stay and fight, or to evacuate," Nate says, ignoring her. "The kibbutz will hold a meeting tonight while you two are out doing your little job."

And then he scrambles out of the room, no doubt to organize everyone else here.

We are pinned down by sniper fire the rest of the day, forced to listen to Zvi's jokes.

"A well-dressed man," says Zvi, "is eating a meal in a restaurant. A woman comes up to him, and very politely says, 'Excuse me, sir, but are you Jewish?'

"'No,' he replies.

"As he's eating his dessert she comes up to him again.

"'Excuse me for bothering you, but are you *sure* you aren't Jewish?'

"'I'm sure.'

"As he's drinking his coffee she approaches him for the third time.

"'Are you absolutely positive you aren't Jewish?' she says.

"'Okay,' he sighs. 'You're right. I'm Jewish.'

"'Funny,' she says, 'you don't look Jewish.'"

Everyone in the room groans. But that doesn't stop Zvi.

"Solly was feeling horrible," Zvi says. "He was light-headed, dizzy, and nauseated. He went to his doctor.

"His doctor had bad news. 'I'm sorry to tell you, but you may have an inoperable brain tumor. Probably you only have a few months left.'

"Solly was devastated. He decided he'd live it up for his last few months on this earth. He spent money on a new car, fabulous food, new clothes. One day he went to get some tailor-made shirts.

"The tailor was fitting him and said, 'You have a seventeen-inch neck.'

"'No,' Solly said. 'I've always worn a fifteen.'

"'Listen,' said the tailor, 'my tape measure doesn't lie. If you tried to wear a fifteen, you'd be light-headed, dizzy, and nauseated!'"

He continues, "This hospital was so crowded that when a patient with double pneumonia came in, they had to turn him away. . . ."

My mind drifts from his jokes and I wonder how I'll do when it comes to actual fighting. Will I have the courage for it? If I have to kill someone, will I be able to? And yet, what choice do I have? If we don't fight, and the Arabs do, we'll all be killed or driven out, or the British will take over again and we'll be under their thumb forever. They could even send me back to Poland. And I know I'd rather die than go back there. I have nowhere else to go, no place else where I am wanted, except here. All I want is to live in peace. But it looks like I'm going to have to fight for that, and maybe die for it. And see my friends die. And maybe—but I can't even let myself think about those really close to me. I'm not sure I could survive if anything happened to them.

I stare at Zvi regaling everyone with his jokes. His eyes are shining, he's lying on the floor with his elbow bent and a hand supporting his head. He's managed to get everyone to think of the stupidest joke they've ever heard.

Finally night comes, the shooting stops, and everyone

gathers for dinner. As soon as we've eaten, Zvi and I get our shovels and head out to what used to be my flower garden, a small flashlight lighting our way. We stop at a tall stake that I had used to mark my wild roses, and count ten steps west. Then we begin to dig. We couldn't mark the spots, of course, in any way that the British might notice. After digging for a good ten minutes, I say to Zvi, "Are you beginning to think that we're in the wrong place?"

"Considering we're halfway to the other side of the world," Zvi remarks, "that wouldn't be a bad assumption."

"This is awful," I exclaim, climbing out of the hole we've dug. "We've lost them!"

"No, that's impossible," Zvi says. "We couldn't have lost them. Are you sure they were ten steps west?"

"Absolutely!"

"Maybe twelve? Or twenty?"

"I'm sure it was ten steps. Zvi, I wouldn't forget! Neither would you."

"Well," says Zvi, "maybe the size of our steps is wrong."

"No, that couldn't be it," I say, remembering. "You counted them."

"Do you have any better idea?" he says, obviously starting to panic.

"No."

"Fine. I'll try again. Taking bigger steps this time."

We go back to the stake and he takes ten long strides. That takes us to just a couple feet farther than the hole we've just dug.

"Zvi," I say, trying to keep how upset I am out of my voice, "what'll we tell everyone if we can't find them?"

"We *will* find them," he says.

Part of me wants to laugh at the silliness of us out here, unable to find the guns, but a bigger part is just plain terrified. After all, without the guns there will be no raid tomorrow, and no way to defend ourselves if the Arabs decide to come down from the hill and mount a real attack. And there's nothing funny about *that* thought.

We start to dig again. The night is cool and a light rain is starting to fall but I'm hot and sweaty. The rain starts to come down harder.

"This is bad," I say.

For once Zvi doesn't have a joke.

"Maybe," I suggest, "we're going in the wrong direction. The flower garden was so tossed around, that stake could be in the wrong spot altogether. Maybe someone stuck it in the ground over there when we were all here singing the other night."

"You're right," Zvi says. He pauses. "But how on earth will we know where it *should* have been?"

Suddenly it occurs to me. "I'll know," I say. "I could've tended that garden in the dark."

"Well," says Zvi, "here's your chance."

We walk back to the garden and I take the flashlight from Zvi. I close my eyes and I imagine the garden exactly as it was. Without opening them I aim the flashlight. "The wild roses should have been right there," I say.

When I open my eyes to look I see that I've located them a good five steps away from where the stake is.

We walk to the spot, measure ten steps, then start to dig again. The rain is pouring down on us, making the digging almost impossible as the light soil quickly turns heavy and hard to manage. Rain runs down my neck into my jersey and soon my trousers are sopping and sticking to me. I try to keep my eyes clear so I can dig but that's impossible. The first heavy rain of winter and it had to be tonight.

Suddenly, though, my shovel hits metal. And so does Zvi's. Wet, filthy, and exhausted, we hug each other and dance around for a minute. Then we finish digging and pull the box out—a dozen rifles. We stagger back to the compound, lugging it between us, and I realize that in a few short hours I'll be carrying one of these guns, going into my first fight.

CHAPTER 6

Before dawn we are all gathered in the dining hall, eight of us, with one gun and ten bullets each. We have four grenades among all of us. Nate tells us that he has successfully scouted where the shooting was coming from, and he describes the four houses we are to attack and disarm.

He leads us through the compound, and up the wooded hill behind Majed. Naturally we aren't going to just walk up the road. It's a bit of a rough climb, and we approach the village from the rear a little too close to sunup—we wanted to attack in complete darkness. We are split into groups, two to take each house. Fortunately the rain has stopped, so at least we don't have to contend with that as well.

I am paired with Karl, who I know must be very torn about this operation. He belongs to the far left group that doesn't believe in partition, but feels the Palestinian Arabs have as much right to be here as we do and that we should all work and live together. I wish it could be like that but I *know* that any ally of Hitler like the Mufti would *never* let that happen. He hates us Jews and he'll be sure to spread that hate as a way for him to get power—power over us and over his own people. Oh, I know him all too well. His friends in Germany killed eighty-eight members of my family.

As I think that, I can feel my fear leave me, and it is replaced by rage. How dare they try to hurt us—fire their guns on women and children. We never did anything to them. The land the kibbutz is on was bought fair and square; it wasn't stolen from anyone.

We creep along the outskirts of the village, moving toward the offending houses. Nate shows Karl and me the house we are to attack. We nod and split off from the group. Karl goes around one side, I go around the other. We listen at the windows. All is quiet. Karl moves toward the door. He motions me to cover him and he uses his foot to kick the door in. It gives way easily and I leap in ahead of him, gun raised, yelling, "Hands up, hands up!" Of course I'm yelling in Hebrew, so the sleepy inhabitants just stare at me. The man on the cot in the back of the dim room reaches for his gun but Karl is too fast for him. He snatches the rifle and looks around to see if there is any more danger. I spot a whole box of bullets near the door. I reach down and pick them up.

We hear firing coming from a house near us. "I've got them," says Karl, gun fixed on the man. "Go check it out."

I hand Karl the box of bullets, then I slip out the door and flatten myself against the front of the house. Right beside me I see Zvi and Fanny pinned down behind an old barrel, being fired on from the house right next to me. Sima is standing uncertainly near the window of the house, grenade in hand.

"Throw the grenade," I yell. "Those two are going to get killed."

"I can't," screams Sima. "I hear a baby crying in there."

I look at the house. The man is firing from the front window but the side window seems clear—he's probably the only armed person in the house. I slip around to the side of the house to the window and peer in. I see one man alone, firing. The mother is in the back of the room, holding a young child who is crying. They look familiar. Then I see Assiya. My heart stops. The mother sees me, warns the man—it's probably Assiya's father! He turns toward me. I raise my gun to shoot but I am frozen, my gun pointed at his chest. How can I shoot her father? Assiya screams, leaps up, throws herself in front of him. He tries to push her out of the way. She struggles. I take advantage of the moment, step away from the window, and flatten myself against the wall. And then, to my overwhelming relief, I see Zvi and Fanny round the corner of the house.

They've obviously slipped away during this lull in the shooting. I motion to them to stand against the wall on the other side of the window when I see the barrel of a gun protruding from the window. Before I even think of what to do Fanny has grabbed the gun with her bare hands. She pulls so hard that she wrenches it free. I hear Assiya's father curse. Assiya pokes her head out of the window. Our eyes lock for a moment. Then I hear Nate, speaking through the bullhorn he's brought along.

"Expel those amongst you who want blood to be shed and accept the hand which is outstretched to you in brotherhood and peace."

That's our signal. It's also the official Haganah message to be delivered to all the villages who will listen. We back away from the houses that we've just disarmed and meet at the edge of the village.

Nate leads us back the way we came and no one pursues us or shoots after us. By the time the sun is finally out from behind the hills, we are back at the kibbutz. Nate sits us down at a table in the dining room to debrief us. A young girl, Danielle, brings us hot tea with lots of sugar. I find that my hands are shaking as I raise my cup.

One by one we tell how our assignments went. When Sima explains why she had refused to throw the grenade, Nate looks grim. He looks furious when I admit I couldn't shoot Assiya's father.

"You both could have cost the lives of Fanny and Zvi," Nate says.

"Our orders are to attack *only* those attacking us," Sima says defiantly. I look at Sima. She's so delicate but I think she's stronger than most of us realize. A survivor of the camps, she rarely speaks but puts all her energy into her art, which is dark and brooding but powerful. I've noticed that lately in each picture she's painted a small ball of light in the corner, a little patch of yellowish white, which I think is her soul shining through all that blackness.

"I think Sima is right," I say. "She couldn't throw the grenade. There was a baby inside that house. And Assiya is my friend. . . .," I add.

"Sima's orders were to throw the grenade if necessary." Nate scowls. "Would you still say she was right if Zvi or Fanny had been killed? You'd probably be at her throat now. And how would you feel if your friend's father killed them and you'd done nothing?"

"I'd feel horrible," I say in a small voice. "I know I should have fired, I just *couldn't*. I was so shocked. I never expected—"

"When we are under attack and we have to retaliate all our training *must* apply," Nate declares. "I know how you feel, Ruth. Imagine how the kibbutzniks feel who have known and been friends with the people in that village all their lives." He pauses. "If Assiya hadn't intervened, you'd probably be dead now. And so would Zvi and Fanny. Think about it. And if you can't do it, let us know now. Before it's too late. We all have to depend on each other."

I feel about two feet tall—and shrinking. I can barely look at anyone. Slowly they all get up from the table and move away. All except Zvi, who is seated beside me.

He looks at the floor for a moment, then he says, "I'm glad you couldn't shoot him, Ruth. It means you're human."

"And if I had shot him—then I *wouldn't* be human, right?" I say.

"No. No. That's not what I meant."

"Because I'll have to shoot people just like him, won't I? It doesn't matter that I don't know their daughters or their sons—they'll still *have* daughters and sons, won't they? And I'll have to kill them, won't I?"

Zvi is silent. He has no answer.

Abruptly I get up from the table. "You said everything here was going to be perfect! You said, you promised, you said *perfect*."

He looks like I've slapped him.

So quietly I can barely hear him, he says, "I thought it would be." He looks up at me. "And it still can be. It *will* be. You'll see."

He reaches out to touch me.

"Leave me alone," I say. And for once I mean it. "Just go away."

Quietly Zvi gets up and leaves the room. Danielle peeks out from the kitchen and brings me some more hot tea. I drink it. And I try not to think.

JANUARY 1948

CHAPTER 7

We sit on the floor in Kibbutz Kfar Etzion as Sima describes the Arab force surrounding us and how they are positioned. It turns out that Sima is not very good at fighting but not because she isn't brave. She just can't bring herself to pull the trigger or lob a grenade. Instead she's become the scout for our section, somehow managing to flit in and out before being caught, often right under the Arabs' noses. I look around the group. We are about to face our biggest test yet, and we're all nervous.

I think back to the last six weeks. We've been in constant action. There was a bit of a lull after our attack on Majed, but shortly after that, our unit was put on convoy duty. Convoys are the only way travel is permitted on those dangerous roads now.

In order to fool the Arabs who lay in wait for the convoys, we'd move on Shabbat or at night or take side roads or dirt roads. We hid guns on us, *not* in pieces like the first time, but tucked into our skirts or blouses, and we returned fire when we could. All we could carry were pistols, though, except Fanny, who actually managed a submachine gun. Meanwhile we were being shot at with rifles and machine guns by the Arabs—not exactly a fair fight. Still, we couldn't let them cut us off from each other—food had to go from the kibbutzim to the cities and people had to travel, too. Jerusalem has been under siege since that first day of the riot, and getting food and supplies through is becoming harder and harder.

In between our convoy duties we've had to go on raids to other Arab villages similar to the one we carried out on

Majed. We've been lucky so far. Although we've had close calls, none of us has been seriously wounded.

I decided that I had to pull myself together, that I couldn't afford to be emotional when we are in action. I try to turn my feelings off and concentrate on the job I've been given, and how to accomplish it with the least bloodshed. I guess it's working, because Nate seems impressed with me. He's made me second in command. The thing is, I still haven't told the truth about my age. I lied when we began our journey from Poland—and now everyone thinks I'm eighteen, when really I'm only sixteen. If they knew the truth, I'd be sitting in the Gadna, the youth troops. I certainly wouldn't be second in command of a Palmach section. I'm counting on Nate *not* to get hurt. I have *no* desire to be commander. In Poland I lied so I wouldn't be treated like a baby—now sometimes I wish I could be.

I know I could drop out of the section, give up fighting altogether, but I can't bring myself to leave my group— someone has to keep Zvi in one piece, after all!

A few weeks after Chanukah, Simon appeared unexpectedly in my tent holding something in his hand. I knew it was a present and I felt bad.

"Simon," I said, "I have nothing for you."

"I'm the big brother," he said solemnly. "I give the presents now."

Tears welled up in my eyes. At Chanukah Father used to give us each a piece of Chanukah gelt, a small coin, so we could buy ourselves a treat. And Mother always gave us chocolate. Simon has become my father and my mother.

He put his hands behind his back. "Choose." He grinned.

I patted his right arm.

"No."

I patted his left arm.

"Wrong again."

"Simon!"

He held out his hand and opened it. Nestled in his palm was a small Star of David dangling on a thin gold chain.

I gasped. "It's so beautiful!"

"A friend of mine made it. Wear it, and remember, soon we'll have our own country."

I kissed him on the cheek. We sat down on Fanny's mat. He told me all about the Irgun's achievements. They'd bombed the Rex, an Arab movie theater in Jerusalem, and they'd set off another device in the Arab market near the Damascus Gate in Jerusalem, all in retaliation for the Arab riots there.

"But Simon," I protested, "those were just regular people you hurt."

"And what were the shopkeepers who were stabbed to death, their stores burned to the ground? Crack Palmach troops?"

"I guess not."

"An eye for an eye, Ruth. They started it. We'll treat them the same as the British. What they do, we'll do, too."

"And what happened in Haifa?" I asked.

"We were retaliating against some Arabs at the oil refinery there. A few were wounded. The rest went crazy and rioted."

"And murdered thirty-nine Jewish workers," I accused him.

"Massacred them," he corrected me.

"You provoked them," I shot back.

"No one can provoke you to murder thirty-nine people," he sighed. "They only had a few wounded, and we were reacting to something *they* had done."

"What?"

He paused and for a minute looked a little uncomfortable. "I don't know. All I know is what I'm told and I trust my leaders, Ruth. They believe in this country more than anyone."

"Oh, Simon, that's silly. Are you telling me that they're better than say, Aunt Sophie, or David Ben-Gurion?"

"Not better maybe, but smarter and more ruthless. They know what it takes to fight evil. You can't be soft, Ruth." He thought for a minute. "I'm worried about you. This policy of the Haganah, only to fight the exact people fighting you—it puts you in terrible danger. I mean, you go into a village, you shouldn't have to worry, I can only shoot this one person, or take that one house. We're at war. All Arabs are our enemies now."

"No!" I exclaimed. "They aren't. Not yet! Maybe this policy will keep the fighting from getting worse. And soon the UN will send troops to enforce the partition. That's what they tell us."

Simon snorted. "That's what they tell you. First of all, the UN is *never* going to send troops here. Second of all, the Haganah is disorganized. Third of all, they can't afford to be so noble. Nobility didn't get us anywhere with Hitler, did it? You can't play fair with people who aren't playing fair back."

The thing is, in a way, I agree with Simon. I mean, to see people shot and killed on those convoys, to be able to do so little to fight back, to clean out a town and find that two days later they're shooting at the kibbutzim again—it's incredibly frustrating. And sometimes, I'm so full of rage and fury I feel I could single-handedly blow them all up without a second thought. Those feelings scare me.

The Haganah position makes logical sense, though, especially if it keeps us from a full-scale war. And even if it doesn't, isn't it worth a try? Then at least we can look back to this time and say that we did everything we could *not* to fight. And why would the UN vote for partition if they didn't mean to enforce it?

I took Simon's hand. "Just don't get hurt. Or arrested," I said.

He kissed me on the cheek. "I'll try. Now I have to go see Rivka."

I grabbed him and give him a big hug. And when he was

gone I felt awful. It doesn't matter that I don't agree with him. He's my older brother. I just don't want anything to happen to him. That's all.

And now our section has been brought south to help defend a block of kibbutzim.

Yitzhak, the Palmach platoon leader, says, "We'll split up into groups. Nate, your section will take the left flank, mine will take the right. Yair, you will also be on the right. Sima, describe what you saw when you were out scouting."

"There are around one thousand Arabs out there," Sima says, "led by Abdel-Kader el-Husseini, the Mufti's cousin. A few hundred women and children have come along, carrying bags to bring home the loot from this kibbutz. A number of the men are sitting around peeling oranges, eating, and waiting for us all to fall over and die." Sima shrugs. "That's it."

"We've been brought in to protect this kibbutz," Nate declares, "and protect it we will."

I look at our group. There are thirty of us. And one thousand of them.

"The kibbutzniks have good defenses set up," he continues, "as you've all seen. They'll be fighting right along with us, defending themselves. All right. Good luck, everyone. Let's move out."

Some people don't even think we should be here defending the kibbutzim in these hills, near Hebron. They're too isolated, too hard to defend, and we could be using our manpower elsewhere. That's what Karl believes. And I've heard that there's been quite a debate over whether or not to spread our resources out, defending everyone, or to concentrate on certain areas. But, since we're here, I guess it's obvious which point of view won out.

I sling my rifle over my shoulder and follow Nate out. Zvi and I do our good luck ritual—we lock our two little fingers, then pull. I'm not sure how it started but now we *have* to do it or we're sure something bad will happen to the other person.

Nate leads our group up the hill so we are flanking the main force of troops. I use the word *troops* loosely. It is mostly the men from all the surrounding villages—and there are lots because this area is almost all Arab. Nate and I climb the hill side by side. "In 1929," he says, "the Arabs rioted and massacred all the Jews of Hebron, then the Jews settled here again and were wiped out again in 1936."

"Thank you, Nate." I grimace. "Just the words of encouragement I needed before going into battle."

Just as we reach our position, the Arab attack begins. There are so many of them, they look so powerful, my heart sinks. I try to put aside the panic I always feel just as we go into action. It's not that I'm afraid for myself. I just can't bear the thought of anyone I care about dying. I've seen that happen too often. I live in terror of something happening to Zvi or to the others. Still, I force myself to put such thoughts aside. If my mind is wandering, I could cause someone to get hurt.

The Arabs begin to run straight for the kibbutz, screaming, "*Jihad, jihad,*" which means "holy war." We wait until they are directly below us in the valley, then open fire. We have a limited supply of bullets, and when that runs out will they slaughter us all, the way the other Jews were killed, time and again? The kibbutzniks have a machine gun and they begin to fire from their dugout. And then, the shout "Jihad" turns to actual screaming and mad confusion. The Arabs begin to retreat! We can't believe it. If they knew how few of us there are!

They regroup and, after what seems like forever, they attack once more. Again, we wait until they are only thirty yards away, then open fire. And again, they retreat! This time Yair takes his group and pursues them, shooting as they go.

"Nate," I say, "they're going in too far. Look, they're almost in the valley!"

Nate sees it as soon as I do. From the hills where the Arabs are running to, a barrage of fire hits Yair's section below us. Yair, his hand raised to signal retreat, is shot. One of his men grabs his body. They are all being shot but they manage to stagger back up the hill helping each other—we Palmachniks *never* leave our wounded on the battlefield. By the time it gets dark we're able to help the wounded back to the compound.

We are almost out of ammunition and we have many wounded. If they should attack again in the morning we'll be finished. Still, for the moment we've managed to pull off a small miracle. Zvi and I lock our little fingers. Someone brings us tea. I go to the large hall we're billeted in and lie down on my blanket. Within seconds I'm asleep, and for once, I don't dream.

CHAPTER 8

The kibbutz has called Jerusalem and begged for reinforcements. Apparently a group of thirty-five Palmachniks has
been dispatched but we begin to worry when night comes
and they haven't arrived. Luckily the Arabs don't attack again,
so we wait. The next day they still haven't arrived and we
spend our time waiting restlessly, no bullets, nothing to do if
we're attacked. On the third day a British convoy pulls up carrying the bodies of all thirty-five fighters. They are horribly
mutilated, their mouths and eye sockets stuffed with their
own amputated body parts. According to the British, the boys
had been spotted in the hills by some of the Arab villagers and
the Arabs quickly surrounded them and attacked. They had
no chance out there, alone. There were no girls in the section—just as well, as they might well have been used first,
then killed. My stomach churns. I try the trick I've learned in
battle: I make my insides stone, because if I allow myself to
feel anything, anything at all, it will be way too much.

Our section stays to bury them, then we are sent back to
Jerusalem, as it looks like, for the moment, the Arabs have had
their revenge and won't attack. Not yet, anyway. But when I
say good-bye to the people on the kibbutz I wonder if they
aren't just committing suicide, staying on a spot where so
much Jewish blood has already flowed. We take advantage of
the British convoy and manage to get back to Jerusalem in
their wake. The kibbutz remains surrounded and under siege.

Our section arrives at Aunt Sophie's a bit like lost souls.
She feeds us cookies and tea as if we're little children. She
even calls us children.

"Children," she says, "I have to tell you I've just come from
a meeting of the High Command and there's been a major

change in policy. We can't, after the deaths of those thirty-five boys, stick to a purely defensive stance. From now on, *any* town or village that is the base for an attack on us is to be attacked—not street by street, either. We are at war and we must behave that way even if it means innocent people may be hurt. However, if a village stays neutral we will not attack it—we will still draw that distinction. Now, I have a job for you. We need an explosives expert. Do you have someone trained as a sapper in your section?"

Rivka raises her hand, just like in school.

"Oh, Rivka," Aunt Sophie says. "Simon's friend."

Rivka smiles.

"I'm glad to see you're still with us, Rivka, and haven't let Simon whisk you off with him."

Rivka turns red. I know that the only reason she's with us is that girls are allowed to fight in the Palmach. And more than anything, Rivka believes that God has given her the right to kill anyone who gets in the way of her people being on this land. I'm not sure but sometimes I think she thinks God *wants* her to kill them because they are so evil. She jumped at the chance to become our sapper and, I must say, she's very good at it.

Aunt Sophie continues. "Our intelligence has found out that a busload of officers, one of *very* high rank in the Arab Liberation Army, is going to cross the border from Lebanon tomorrow. We want that bus blown up. You'll move out tonight in a couple of jeeps, using back roads that Jonathan has mapped out for you. He'll also supply you with explosives and more bullets for your guns. Meantime you can bunk down here, in my dining room."

A short while later Jonathan arrives, and he, Nate, and I go over the roads and our strategy. When we're finished I sneak off to Aunt Sophie's office to have a moment alone with her.

"Have you heard from Simon?" I ask.

She shakes her head. "They should join us now," she says. "We don't need their terrorist tactics anymore."

"*Anymore,* Aunt Sophie," I exclaim, pretending to be shocked. "Do you mean you ever did?"

She gives me a wan smile and chuckles. "Caught me there. Well, now they are *certainly* no use—they should join the regular army and get trained. They don't know how to fight, only how to throw bombs and run away. What good will that be when *real* war comes and *real* armies are bearing down on us? Then we'll need all the help we can get."

"I agree with you, Aunt Sophie," I say. "I don't need to be convinced. I have to say this about Rivka: She's practical that way. She's made sure she's in a unit where she can fight."

Just then the phone rings and Aunt Sophie shrugs an apology to me. I give her a quick kiss.

The jeeps are loaded and we pile in. Nate drives one, Miriam the other. The roads are awful. We bump and lurch along all night. We're lucky we don't encounter any Arabs but perhaps it's no surprise, as half the time I wonder if we're actually on a road at all. By morning it is pouring rain, and we reach our destination cold and shivering. Nate and Miriam hide the jeeps, and we march down the road in the downpour until we find the curve that Jonathan had marked on the map. Rivka will plant the explosives so that as the bus rounds the curve, it will be pushed sideways by the explosion and, hopefully, drop off the steep embankment there. Rivka gets to work on the explosives, with me helping her. I think she likes to make me do this just so she can boss me around. Also she knows I don't like working with the stuff—it makes me nervous.

We have to plant the charge on the uphill side of the road in order for the bus to be thrown toward the precipice. And since we can't string the wire across the road in case they see it, we are forced to find a place on the embankment side from which to detonate the explosion. The road has a small stone wall along the embankment, and a few yards beyond that, right at the bend in the road, is a large pile of stones. This is a perfect place for us to hide after we've placed the explosives.

Rivka finishes her work, then goes to the other side of the road to make sure it's not too visible. Nate and the others are also on the far side of the road. If the bus doesn't fall off the embankment, they will open fire.

Suddenly I hear the sounds of gravel crunching and back-fires from an engine. The bus must be early. Rivka motions madly at me, then dives down for cover with the others. I realize with horror that I am staring at the detonator button and will have to push it as the bus crosses over the explosives.

The bus comes into view and from an open window I hear a woman talking loudly. A woman. I look at the button. What if it's the wrong bus? This bus should be filled only with Arab officers. The bus gets closer and closer. And what if it's the right bus and I let it pass? The image of the mutilated bodies of the thirty-five Palmachniks passes before my eyes. I've tried not to think about it, I haven't cried, none of us have talked about it, but the thought keeps popping up, that could have been me, or him, or her, and I think of the camps and I think of the smell of death, and disease, and rotting. I look up at the bus. It is right over the explosives. I push the button.

Nothing happens.

Time seems to stretch and for a moment I am frozen and then I press it again but still nothing when suddenly a shot rings out. I see the bus driver slump over. Someone has shot him. The bus screeches ahead, lurches from side to side, and comes to a stop just above me. I am hidden by the wall and the rocks.

And then all hell breaks loose. My unit opens fire on the bus and those in the bus fire back. I look up to see an Arab fighter leap out of the open bus door. He runs onto the top of the wall then jumps from the wall down to the ground just level with me, in order to escape the fire from my unit.

My heart stops. I realize that this is their only means of escape. And I am the only one here. The Arab fighter sees me as soon as he is on the same level as me. I pick up my Sten gun. I aim, but it jams! He fires, and a bullet whizzes past my ear. I pick up Rivka's rifle, pull the bolt, aim, and fire. The Arab screams and falls backward. But another one has just jumped down from the wall and is looking around. I fumble for a bullet, reload, pull the bolt, aim, fire again. This one falls too.

They are all trying to get out of the line of fire.

Another leaps down, this one firing as he runs. I reload, pull the bolt, aim, fire. They are pouring out of the bus now, and all I can think, while I reload, pull the bolt, aim, and fire, reload, pull the bolt, aim, and fire, is how lucky I am to have ammunition. But maybe I still won't have enough, because soldiers keep pouring out of the bus and surely I'll be dead soon, anyway. Reload, bolt, aim, fire. Again. Reload. Bolt. Aim. Fire. Again. Again. Again. A fighter runs toward me, scream-ing. I fire. He falls forward. He is quiet. For a moment, there is complete silence. No more soldiers jump from the bus.

The firing has stopped from across the road, too. A woman starts to cry in the bus. Then Rivka jumps down from the road and runs over to me. She doesn't say anything; she appears to be speechless. She checks to see if I'm unhurt. I think I am. She scrambles up the rocks to the bus. Then Zvi is beside me but I can't let go of the rifle, he has to pry it out of my hands. I stand. Nate is counting.

"Sixteen," he says. "Sixteen. All dead. Including the man we were after."

They are all staring at me.

I stare back. No one speaks.

CHAPTER 9

I still can't quite comprehend what just happened, but maybe it's good I have no time to think about it. The minute our section arrives back in Jerusalem, we are given our old job back as guards and put on a convoy heading for Tel Aviv. Aunt Sophie promises that after we get the convoy back from Tel Aviv, with supplies, then we can take the next one to our kibbutz for one day of leave.

They've tried to make the cars and trucks in the convoys a little safer, but that's balanced out by the better organization on the Arab side. Abdel-Kader, who is in charge of the Arabs living along this stretch of highway, has obviously developed a pretty efficient system, because they are always ready for us, no matter when we move.

We have homemade armored cars now. We call them sandwiches because they are covered with steel, then a layer of wood, then another layer of steel. The firing slits on them are very large, though, and make an easy target for the Arabs. On the trucks, the drivers are protected in their cabs by some armor plating—but it won't stop machine gun or cannon fire.

We don't bother to go to sleep because it's best to drive at night, so we leave at around eleven. We hit one roadblock, an open ditch that we have to fill up with dirt so the cars and trucks can get over it. I stand guard while the rest shovel, although I can't see a thing, it's so pitch dark. We manage the rest of the trip without incident. The most nerve-racking part of the drive is the worry about mines. If one goes off under you—well, that's probably it, and there's no way to fight back.

We set off midafternoon on the return trip to Jerusalem so

we'll reach Bab el Wad by nightfall. A mine goes off about a half hour out of Tel Aviv and hits the car in front of us. Zvi is in that car, which lifts off the ground. Since it's not a direct hit, it falls back in one piece and continues on. My stomach turns over and I try to catch my breath. In front of Zvi is Nate in the lead truck, equipped with bulldozer blades so he can move any roadblocks we encounter. Rivka is riding beside him, sten gun ready. Karl is driving our car. We have three passengers in the back. Just behind us is a truck with a driver and Sima in the cabin; just behind Sima is another truck with Miriam driving and Fanny as the escort. Passengers are crammed in wherever there is room. The trucks are crammed with flour, rice, sugar, and, underneath it all, guns and ammunition.

We sing songs to try to keep our minds off the danger, which is everywhere, but as we reach the sixteen-mile stretch of road from Bab el Wad to Jerusalem, our singing dies. All is silent. The skies have cleared and the moon and stars shed some light. We enter the deep ravine, rocks and fir trees rising up like the ghosts and demons I used to tell about in the stories I often made up for my brothers and my sister. Suddenly there is a flash and a grenade explodes just in front of our car. The convoy slows. I suspect we've hit a roadblock, maybe an old car or something else dragged onto the road. I can see shapes moving among the rocks. I aim, then fire. Aim again, fire.

Nate's truck must have moved the roadblock, because we're able to travel a little faster now, all of us returning fire as we can. But suddenly there is a terrible explosion and I see through a slit in the back that the truck behind us, with Sima in it, has taken a direct hit from a grenade. There is a white cloud forming over it as the flour rises into the air.

That's good cover, I think to myself, like fog. Without taking time to think I leap out of the car, Karl yelling at me to come back, and firing my gun at the shadowy figures in the rocks I race back to Sima's truck. I pry open the door. Sima is slumped forward, burned, unconscious. The driver is dead. I grab Sima and throw her over my shoulder. She's only about a hundred pounds but I'm not that big myself. I guess I have to thank Nate, after all, for those horrible early morning runs with fifty-pound packs on our backs, because Sima right now doesn't feel like more than that. I race back to our car. Out of the corner of my eye I notice Fanny covering me with her rifle, even as Miriam backs the truck up. They won't be able to get past Sima's truck, and I just hope they can turn around or they'll be caught for sure. I don't even want to think about what might happen to them if they are captured—they would probably turn their guns on themselves before that happened.

I throw Sima onto the seat, slam the door, and start firing again. There is another flash up ahead but since we keep moving I assume the grenade didn't hit exactly on target.

The convoy is inching up the hills in low gear. Our fierce counterfire must be having an effect, because the shooting seems to be lessening.

"Please, I'm a nurse," says our only female passenger. "Can I get a look at her?"

She leans over the front seat.

"She's breathing," says the nurse. "But she's burned terribly, and I think she must have a concussion. She needs a hospital, badly." She pauses. "Is there anything here I can use—a first aid kit?"

"Only that blanket on the floor," I say.

"Wrap her up," the nurse instructs me, "but really, there is nothing to do but try to get her some real help."

A man sitting next to the nurse mutters, "This the last time I'm making this trip, I don't care what they say."

"Let's just hope it isn't our last time altogether," says the nurse.

I cover Sima with the blanket and position her so her head

leans on my shoulder. It feels like we are going about two miles an hour. It feels like we will never get out of these hills. But the attack has stopped for the moment, a good thing since, naturally, I am almost out of ammunition.

After an hour or so, I start to nod off and am awakened by Sima suddenly thrashing about and screaming.

I try to quiet her—both for her own good and for ours. We don't need any Arabs hearing those screams, but Sima doesn't understand. She's in too much pain.

"We have to keep her quiet," Karl says. "She'll give the whole convoy away."

Quickly I untie the cotton strip I have around my head to keep my hair out of my eyes. The nurse leans over and holds Sima while I tie it around Sima's head and over her mouth as a gag. When I touch her face, some of her skin just peels right off in my hand. I don't want to be gagging her, I want to be soothing her and helping her! Tears slip down my cheeks, but I have to restrain her or risk the rest of the convoy.

Sima is in so much pain that she really doesn't know where she is or what is happening—delirious, I suppose. After a few minutes she sinks back into unconsciousness, the pain probably too much to bear. I hold her against me as gently as I can.

Finally we arrive in Jerusalem. Sima is taken out of my arms. An ambulance rushes her to the hospital; the rest of us gather in a billet in the New City. We are fed and given places to sleep, but none of us want to go to bed. We sit up, drinking tea, Nate calling the hospital every hour. Just before dawn they tell him that Sima has died.

The funeral will be today.

CHAPTER 10

Nate is going crazy with worry over Miriam, and insists our section take the first convoy out, back to the kibbutz. Aunt Sophie had promised us that we could at any rate, but now with the funeral the rest of us won't leave.

Nate puts me in charge of the section and goes with the convoy. I call Aunt Sophie and ask her if we can bury Sima in the old fig grove behind her house—it's so beautiful and peaceful there. She agrees and assures me that she'll have the body brought to the house. We make our way there, get our shovels, and dig a grave about halfway up the hill.

An ambulance arrives with Sima's body. No one has had time to arrange for a casket. She is wrapped in a white shroud. We lay her gently in the ground. Everyone looks at me, as section head, to say something.

"The first time I noticed Sima," I say, "was when we were leaving Poland. We were on the train. She began to sing. She'd somehow survived the concentration camps and she sang a song she'd learned there. The song describes a girl who dreams she wakes up in a land of palaces, beautiful gardens, birds singing. But when the dreamer really wakes up, she is in a concentration camp. The chorus goes:

> It is a lie
> It is a lie
> It is a useless dream
> There is no palace in the desert, no field,
> no trees."

I pause.

"But you see, Sima, there is a place of beauty, of trees, and birds. And you got to see it before you died. And you loved it so much you were willing to die for it—even though you could never hurt another human being. Still, for some reason, God chose you to die, you who only wanted to sing, and to draw and to create love and beauty.

"You had to die in agony, your mouth gagged so the Arabs couldn't hear your screams. You had no family left, Sima. They were killed by the Nazis. And now another enemy up in the hills has finished what the Nazis started." Tears are burning my eyes. "Rest in peace, Sima. Now you can rest. You wanted"— my voice breaks—"we all wanted *this* to be paradise, our land, Eretz Israel, but you'll have to settle for a different paradise. May the angels take special care of you."

Aunt Sophie recites the kaddish. There is only one shovel, so we take turns throwing dirt over Sima's body until the grave is full.

Then we weep, arms around each other. We weep for ourselves and our loss. We weep for her family, too—because now that she is gone, the last of a huge family, they, too, are dead forever. And *I* can't help but weep for Mother and Father and Joshua and Hannah. We are all orphans here. It's times like these I'm sorry I can feel anything because my heart hurts—it hurts.

When we ride on the convoy the next day, guns ready, my mouth is dry. I can barely swallow as our car twists and turns through the mountain roads. And then we see it, the truck Sima had been in, pushed to the side of the road, already looted by the Arabs, a ghostly shell of twisted metal. I won't cry again. I can't. I have to be on the lookout, to be sure that it won't happen to any of us.

We finally arrive at Kibbutz David and we find Nate, Fanny, and Miriam. Fanny and Miriam somehow had managed to get their truck turned around. Although Fanny was shot in the arm, it's not a serious wound and, knowing her, she'll be fine in a week.

I'm so relieved to find them alive that I feel almost dizzy. I can't remember when I last slept but I'm not at all tired. I go find my garden, or what used to be my garden. The sky has cleared and the sun is warm today. It heats me as I sit amongst my broken flowers and plowed-up dirt. And then I get up, grab a shovel, and begin to turn the soil over. I mash the broken stems and petals into the soft earth and I dig and turn until sweat pours down my face. At some point Zvi shows up and he gets a shovel and starts to help. Then Fanny, using one arm, and Nate and Miriam and Karl and even Rivka. We stop only to drink water, and after a while Fanny starts to sing an old Yiddish nursery rhyme. We all join in.

> On the little hearth
> A lively fire burns
> Casting warming rays
> As the Rebbe teaches
> All the little ones.
> And if, God forbid,
> This land casts us out,
> We will find new hope.
> Golden words we've learned
> Will be a source of strength
> And teach us how to cope.

From nursery rhymes Fanny turns to folk songs, and we sing at the tops of our lungs.

By the time the sun sets, we're filthy and exhausted and hungry, but my garden is ready to be replanted. We go to the dining hall and gobble down all the food offered and then fight over who's to shower first.

Finally, I sink onto my cot, clean, full, and tired, and I fall asleep.

I wake up screaming. Fanny is shaking me but I still see them coming at me, out of the bus, one by one, and I fire and they scream and another one lunges at me and I fire and they scream, and they won't stop.

"Wake up!" Fanny is yelling.

I am awake, but I can still see them. I run to the back of the tent to get away from them but they won't stop coming at me. Fanny leaves me and I hear her calling to someone and I am cringing in the corner when Morris arrives. I see him, but I also see my victims. How can that be?

Gently, he takes my arm, and gives me an injection. I start to feel heavy, and sleepy, and my eyes close and the images go away. When I wake up I'm in a bed in the infirmary. Morris is sitting and reading in a chair beside the bed.

He sees me open my eyes.

"What happened?" I ask.

"You had a waking dream," he answers. He pats my hand. "Don't worry, you're not going crazy. I understand none of you has slept for a while. It's quite common when your sleep patterns are disturbed." He looks at me. "What did you see?"

"The Arabs I killed."

"Sixteen, I was told," Morris says, eyebrows raised. "That's quite an accomplishment."

"Is it?"

"You'll be a heroine."

"I don't want to be a heroine for killing people," I say, near tears. "I had no choice. They were coming at me. Our orders were to destroy the bus and the people on it, but the explosives wouldn't work, probably because it was wet. I trained and trained; when the enemy runs at you with a gun, you shoot."

"What else should you have done?" Morris asks.

"I don't know," I say.

"You had no choice."

"Didn't I?"

"Not then."

"But when I became a fighter," I say, "then I had a choice, right?"

"You did," he nods. "You could have gone to live in a youth village."

I sit up. "You know?"

"That you're younger than you claim to be? Yes."

I stare at him. He's in his thirties, very thin. His face almost looks as though there are hollows carved into it. He's from Poland, too, but he came here before the war started and now he's married and has two children. He's always very calm and he can be funny, too, if you pay attention.

"How do you know?"

"I'm a doctor. I gave you your physical when you first got here."

"But I'd been in the camps. My growth was stunted. You *couldn't* tell. . . ."

"You're right." He grins. "I couldn't. I overheard you bullying Zvi. You made him promise not to tell your real age, which was fifteen. And now you're sixteen. You should be in the Gadna, the youth troops, not second in command of a Palmach unit."

"Pretending I was older kept me alive," I state.

"And now it could get you killed."

For a moment, neither of us speaks.

"It's not too late," he says. "You can admit your age. No shame in it. They'll transfer you to a youth village, or even make you a leader in the Gadna. Do you know what you're in for, otherwise?"

"What?"

"Shortly, the Haganah will stop being purely defensive. They'll have to go on the offense. And who will they send? You Palmachniks. You'll constantly be in action. Can you take it?"

"I don't know." I pause. "I can't just leave my group. They depend on me."

"You'll be no use to them if you fall apart."

My eyes meet his. He nods. I know he's right.

"How do I know if I can take it or not?" I ask.

He grins. "That's a good question. I'll tell you. If you can't sleep, if you have horrible nightmares, if you feel depressed, those are all warning signs."

"But Morris," I protest, "I've been like that since the war ended."

He looks at me thoughtfully. "That's true."

"And when I'm doing what I can with my group, at least I don't feel"—I search for the word—"helpless."

"Ah," he says.

I try to think it through. "You see, if I went and sat in a youth village or did nothing I'd feel like I used to feel in the camps, but now—well, I might die, but I won't die like some poor frightened animal. I'll die fighting. And"—now that I'm talking I can't stop—"it's not like I'd necessarily be safe somewhere else. A children's village can get bombed; I could get killed living anywhere. We're all targets." I pause. "We'll have to fight until we're safe."

He nods again. "All right, Ruth. I won't give away your secret. Why should I? You can do the job as well as anyone, better than most. But you have to promise me that if it gets too much for you, you'll let me know. I can always put you on sick leave for a week or two."

"You can?"

"Yes."

"Well then, there is something that would make me feel better."

"What's that?"

"I need a couple of days to plant my garden again."

"You've got it. In fact, I'll put your entire section on leave for two days. I think you deserve it."

"Thank you." I smile at him.

"Your whole face changes when you smile," he says. "You should try it more often. I have a theory that if you smile first, you'll feel better after."

"That's Zvi's theory, too," I say to him as I get up from the bed. "A joke for every occasion."

"Yes," Morris says, "but some of Zvi's jokes are enough to make you cry."

Impulsively I give him a hug. He hands me a flashlight and I make my way back to the tents. When I get back I see Zvi has fallen asleep on my cot.

"Are you all right?" Fanny asks.

"I'm fine," I say as I slide into bed beside Zvi and wake him with a kiss that has so much passion in it, I feel like I could devour him with it. He wakes and responds in kind. I hear Fanny say, "Well, I can see where I'm not wanted." And she leaves.

I want to do everything with Zvi, I want to be one with him so badly, but he stops and he gasps, "Ruth, we can't."

We are both gasping.

I know he's right—some fighter I'd make if I got pregnant.

"I love you," he says, and he holds me, tight.

"I love you, too," I reply. "Now get out of here before I lose all my willpower."

He slips away and Fanny returns. "Wonderful night's sleep I'm getting," she says sourly. But Fanny can never stay mad at anyone. I think back to what Morris said.

"Do you think I'm a heroine, Fanny?" I say.

"More like a lunatic," she replies.

"That's what I think," I say and, somehow, I fall straight to sleep.

APRIL 1948

CHAPTER 11

I check my gun one last time, getting ready for our new mission. I think back to my talk with Morris, the night I had the waking nightmare. He'd been right. After our two days of leave we *were* taken off road duty and were given missions that consisted of sorties into Arab villages from which Arabs were mounting raids. We no longer simply disarmed the village, but we tried to take over the town and hold it until reinforcements came. Sometimes reinforcements didn't arrive for days, sometimes we were left without food or water for days. The Hebrew word *balagan* seemed to describe it best for everyone. A big mess. Chaos.

We had to go back to Majed, the Arab village overlooking our kibbutz. This time we took the entire village because they had been shooting at the kibbutz again, making it impossible to work the fields, or even to move safely from building to building. After we'd taken our objectives, almost all the residents fled—even though we assured them that they could stay on. Now it lies empty.

I try not to think about Assiya, but it's hard. Where will she go? What will happen to her and to her family? Why did they have to leave? Why couldn't we share this land? It reminds me so much of the war—everyone was forced to be different. The Nazis split everyone up into groups so they'd hate each other—Jews, Communists, Poles, Gypsies. After all, if you realize that another group is really very much like your group, why fight? The Mufti has tried to make us seem like devils to the Arabs, devils that will kill them. In the few months after our first raid to Majed, we had no more trouble. I used to dream that maybe we'd be the example for everyone in

Palestine—how an Arab village and a Jewish kibbutz could live peacefully, side by side. That dream is over.

Harvey, a young volunteer from Canada, joined our section to replace Sima, but he was killed only a few weeks after he joined us. After that, Joe and Zach, both Americans, were sent to join us and they've both fit in well. We are getting ready for a dangerous mission into Arab territory—but I know that I couldn't be with a better, more disciplined, well-trained troop. If anyone can pull this off, we can.

I'm sure Aunt Sophie didn't want us for this mission but we are the natural choice, being the Palmach section based near Ramle, where the operation is to take place. This is a job for Rivka, and I'm sure she's up to it.

We miss Sima, of course—not only as our friend but as our scout. Zach has taken over her job. Small, blue-eyed, and blond, he's very fast and seems to be able to move at twice the speed of the rest of us. He has scouted the building, a two-story brick house set back in an orange grove, which houses the Mufti's area commander and all the support personnel. We are targeting them because in two days Operation Nachshon begins, the biggest operation yet. Fifteen hundred troops will be brought together to open up the Tel Aviv–Jerusalem road and break the siege of Jerusalem. The operation is named after Nachshon, who is said to be the first person to step into the Red Sea when Moses parted it as the Israelites were escaping from bondage in Egypt. With Passover approaching, I guess it's a good code name.

Since this Arab area commander will be mounting raids on the highway and organizing all the villages in this area, it will help to take him out of action and create a little chaos in their leadership.

Nate checks that we are all ready. We slip into the fields after him, through our cotton plants, then down dirt paths. It takes us at least three hours, but finally we arrive at our destination. Guards are posted all along the citrus grove, and we have each been assigned one—to kill. We split up and I head for my target, the guard who is watching the road just beyond the grove. I move slowly, silently, concentrating only on not stepping on a twig or brushing against any leaves, which might make a rustling sound. It is dark, but there is a moon, so I have enough light to see by. Finally I spot him. He's leaning against a tree, gun by his side, peeling an orange. I wish he weren't eating. You can avoid thinking of your enemy as a human like you, maybe with a wife, or children, or parents who love him, if he stands gun in hand, ready to shoot you. But eating—everyone eats. They should just get the two armies together and let them eat each other's oranges— maybe then no one would want to fight.

I try to shut my mind off. It often wanders like this just before we have to go into action. This is different, though. I really don't want to think about what I have to do. Battle is one thing. You're fighting someone who is shooting at you. But this fellow isn't shooting at me. He would be, of course, if he saw me, but that doesn't seem to help.

I pull the knife out of the sheath which is strapped to my leg. I find my hand is shaking. My breath is coming in short gasps. Why did Aunt Sophie have to choose us? At this moment I hate her. I am supposed to slip the knife into his back, between his ribs, so it'll puncture his heart. My gun is slung over my shoulder.

I creep up behind him. He doesn't hear me. At the last moment, I slip my knife back into its sheath and drop my gun off my shoulder. Raising it, I swing it fast and hard into the guard's head. I hear a sickening thud and the guard drops to the ground. I bend over him. He's out, but he's breathing.

I'm glad he's not dead. I can't become a cold-blooded killer. I can't stab someone in the back. My hands are still shaking as I pick up his gun and sling it over my other shoulder. Gingerly I pick my way through the grove until I meet up with the others.

Rivka motions to me. She still insists I be her assistant,

despite my objections. She has already planted the bomb. I help her string the wire but my hands won't stop shaking. We're using a long fuse as it'll give us more time to escape. We've eliminated the guards as a threat but not the garrison, which is encamped on the north side of the building. Rivka lights the fuse. We move back into the grove and take cover. Within a minute there is a huge explosion and when we look, it seems like almost the entire building has crumpled. Nate leads us back the way we came and in all the yelling and confusion we are able to escape without any counterattack. I am weak with relief. If that guard I hit had woken up and sounded the alarm, the entire mission would have been ruined. We all could have been killed. Because I wasn't able to follow my orders.

So this is what Simon and the Irgun do every day. I could never do it. Our target was a military target, but sometimes the Irgun attacks civilian targets. How do they do it? What do they *feel* inside? Do they ever think about the people they are hurting? Maybe not. Maybe all they can think about is how their people have been hurt and how they will get revenge, fight back. An eye for an eye. Am *I* too soft? Or are they too hard?

We get back to the kibbutz at dawn. Varda hands Nate a message. Our section is to join the larger battalion the next morning. A whole day to recuperate! It feels like we've been given a wonderful gift. Often over the last six or eight weeks we would go two or three nights without sleep. We would take a target and have to hold it until the regular Haganah would come in and relieve us. By then we would be beyond exhaustion.

We all tumble into our tents and I sleep most of the day, waking just before dinner to go check my garden. The annuals are flowering already because of all the rain we've had and by this summer I think the new garden will be even more beautiful than the old one.

As I do a little weeding, Zvi turns up, like he always does.

He grins at me. I know what's coming.

"A rabbi and a priest are sitting together on a first-class train. The porter comes down the aisle and asks if he can get them something to drink.

"The rabbi says, 'Certainly, I'll have a schnapps.'

"'And you, sir?' the porter says to the priest.

"The priest is horrified. 'Young man, before I touch any alcohol, I'd just as soon commit adultery.'

"'Oh,' says the rabbi, 'as long as there's a choice, I'll have what he's having.'"

I laugh, and Zvi looks pleased with himself.

"Joe just told me that one," he says.

Joe, who joined us when Zach did, is a U.S. soldier who fought in the war and then came over here to help. He's a real tough guy, just like in the American movies I've seen in Jerusalem, and he and Zvi regale each other with jokes all the time. His are often pretty crude. But Zvi picks out the better ones for me.

"I have another," he says. I listen as I work.

"Paul, who is Catholic, brags to his friend Moishe, 'My priest knows more than your rabbi.'

"'Of course he does,' Moishe scoffs, 'you *tell* him everything.'"

That gets a smile.

"One last one," says Zvi.

"All right."

"One day Mordechai goes to visit a psychiatrist.

" 'Doctor,' he says, 'something terrible has happened. I can see the future! Before something even happens, I know it's *going* to happen!'

"The doctor nods and says, 'When did you first notice this?'

"'Next Monday!'"

"You and Joe are a bad influence on each other," I say. "I'm the one who wants to be a bad influence on you." I smile.

At that Zvi grabs me, pulls me to him, and kisses me. I hold him tight.

"I've missed you," he says.

"I've missed you, too," I whisper.

Of course, we see each other every day, every night. But we have no time to talk, to dream together, just to *be*.

"Big operation tomorrow," he says, pulling me down on the ground beside him.

"Yes."

"Ruth, if something should happen to me—"

"It won't!"

"Ruth, I know how hard it would be on you—only I don't want you ever to give up. You have to promise me."

I look into his eyes. "I can't."

"You have to." He pauses. "Or I'll tell."

"You'll tell what?"

"That you're only sixteen. They won't let you fight then."

"We all fudged our age to get into the Palmach," I remind him. "You don't turn eighteen until May, do you?"

"Well," he scoffs, "that's not a big difference."

"It was a year ago when we started training," I said. "You tell on me, I'll tell on everyone else."

He sighs. "You have to promise."

"I can't," I reply stubbornly. "Can you?"

He takes a deep breath. "Yes. Yes. I promise."

I smack him. "That's romantic. You promise you'll carry on without me. Thanks a lot, Zvi."

He looks hurt. "Wouldn't you want me to?"

"No, I'd want you to die of a broken heart."

"I probably would," he mutters.

"What's that?"

"Nothing."

"I think we should both swear that we'll die of broken hearts if anything happens to the other one," I say. "And," I continue softly, "and try our best not to. But no promises."

"One day," Zvi says, putting my hands in between his two large warm ones, "we'll marry. And we'll have children. And they'll play in this garden, Ruth."

"Not in my garden, they won't! And trample my flowers!"

"You're right, of course." Zvi grins. "They'll play in the playground with the other children."

"And they won't ever have to suffer what we did," I say fiercely. "They'll be safe here. And gas ovens and camps will just be some horrible nightmare that happened so long ago. And they'll love it here not because they have nowhere else, but because it's home."

"And they'll grow up in the kibbutz sharing everything and we'll show the world a new way. We will, Ruth. You'll see."

It scares me more than anything—dreams. I've never *dared* to have them. I feel that just for talking like this a bolt of lightning will come and strike me down. But it doesn't. So Zvi and I kiss, and hold each other tight, and do the unimaginable—dream of the future.

CHAPTER 12

We've been fighting for three days on Operation Nachshon when I'm called away. One convoy has already gotten through to Jerusalem successfully. Our section has managed to take two Arab villages. We also heard today that Kastel, a very important village overlooking the highway, was taken, then lost. The leader, Abdel-Kader el-Husseini, was shot, though, and the Arabs were so demoralized that they ran off, so Kastel is now back in Jewish hands.

When we go back to the kibbutz for a short rest, I am given a message from Aunt Sophie. Somehow she has arranged for me to get into Jerusalem on a British jeep, of all things! Nate is furious.

"Your aunt Sophie can't just take my second in command. I need you!"

"So does she apparently," I say. "Look, Nate, I'll rejoin you as soon as I can, but Aunt Sophie wouldn't pull me out for nothing."

Nate turns to Zvi. "You'll be second then, Zvi, until Ruth gets back. Let's go."

Zvi grabs my finger with his. We do our little ritual. A moment to look at each other, and he's gone.

Sure enough, a British jeep stops and picks me up at the entrance to the kibbutz.

I ride in the back. The two privates in front completely ignore me. They speak English, of which I can only catch snatches. The ride goes so quickly compared to our rides in the convoys when we are under attack at every second. It's hard to believe it's the same trip. We arrive at Aunt Sophie's without incident.

She meets me at the door with a big hug. "Come in, dear, come in." Her house is packed with people, phones are ringing, messengers are running in and out. "Such a big operation," she says. "So much to do. But I'm glad I could get you here. Nice that so many British soldiers need money these days."

She sits me down in a chair. "It's the Irgun," she says.

"Simon isn't hurt?"

"No, he's not hurt. But apparently Lehi have decided that they want to fight in this operation."

I shake my head. Lehi, sometimes called the Stern gang, are even more violent than the Irgun. I guess I should be happy Simon doesn't belong to them, as they are real fanatics.

"They want to help open this road," Aunt Sophie says. "So they went to the Irgun and the two groups have joined together. They've decided to capture a town, Deir Yassin. We've tried to convince them that there are other towns far more important to us, but they won't listen! In fact, the inhabitants of Deir Yassin are neutral; they've never attacked us. Still, it *is* near the Jerusalem road and since we can't stop them anyway, we've told them that if they *do* take it, they'll have to hold it—no use just going in, disarming them, and leaving. So, this is where you come in. They've agreed to let us send an observer along. They've never trusted us, as you know, but you are acceptable since you're Simon's sister. They figure you won't betray them to the British—as if any of us would!

"At any rate, we want you to observe them from a military standpoint. Can they fight? How easy will it be to integrate them into our army? Remember: The British leave next month and then we'll have to have one army, all under one command. They begin their attack tonight. They've told us where you can meet them, in Bet Hakerem. All that's left is for you to say *yes.*"

"And if I say no?" I ask, teasing.

"Then I suppose a court-martial will be in order."

I nod solemnly. "Then I'll have to say yes. Actually I wouldn't mind seeing Simon in action."

"Fine. Now, can you find a corner to hide in, dear? I have so much to do."

There are no corners free so I go out to Sima's grave and sit. I can hear gunfire, see smoke both on the road and in the city. The convoy that just got through was the first one in weeks. A smell from the city wafts in, of rot, unwashed people, and toilets with no water to flush, all mixed up with the sweet scent of flowers that are growing madly everywhere because of the rains and no one to cut them. Aunt Sophie told me that people have been forced to cook weeds for food.

In February a bomb went off on Ben Yehudah Street. At least fifty Jews were killed. And in March the Jewish Agency was bombed. The city has really gone through so much but it isn't the only place under siege. One of our youth villages has been under siege for a couple of months now, as have so many kibbutzim. Everything is a mess, and although I can see when I'm here that High Command is trying to organize, when you're out there it feels like nothing is coordinated at all.

When night falls, I make my way through the streets of the suburb. It's quiet but that doesn't mean a sniper couldn't pick me off at any time. I meet up with Simon and the others. We are to follow an armored car they've stolen from the British which is equipped with a loudspeaker. They plan to warn the villagers of the attack and to encourage them to run away without a fight. Simon explains this all quickly to me.

"Our commander, Yaacov, is brilliant. We'll have the town in an hour and that'll show the Haganah that we are real fighters! We're out to prove ourselves to everyone today!" His eyes are gleaming.

"Simon," I caution him, "taking a village is different from just throwing a bomb and running away. You have to know how to fight, how to do it! I trained for a year before I saw action. You haven't trained at all!" I can't help but think about the bomb we set off near Ramle, and how different that operation was from our regular ones.

"It'll be easy," Simon scoffs. "Now come on. I'm counting on you for a good report."

"I'll report what I see, Simon."

He stares at me. "Well, aren't we just too grown-up!"

I'm exhausted from the last three days of fighting and in no mood for Simon to try to bully me.

"Yes. Well, *I* am," I retort. "I'm not so sure about you." I pause. "Have you seen how this city is suffering? How badly it needs supplies? Well, the first convoy in weeks just got through, no thanks to the Irgun. Operation Nachshon was almost ruined by that bomb you set off near Tel Aviv."

Simon grins. "That was a successful little operation."

"You may think so, but the British were so mad, they closed the roads around Tel Aviv to try to find the bombers. We couldn't get the guns we needed, which were coming from Tel Aviv. Finally, they arrived just in time or the entire operation would have been scrapped. And don't you think this operation is more important than what you did? You should be working *with* the central command."

"Right," he says sarcastically. "If it wasn't for us, those Limeys wouldn't even be leaving."

"That's what *you* say."

"Are you two ready?" Yaacov interrupts us. "Well, at least I can see she's not a Haganah plant. Only a real sister would behave that way to her brother!"

I almost stick out my tongue at him and catch myself just in time! Not exactly the sort of thing a mature fighter would do.

We leave at around two A.M. Not long after, we encounter a trench on the road, obviously dug by Arabs. This group has brought no shovels—standard equipment in our missions, as you often encounter this type of roadblock—so we all have to pitch in with hands, helmets, whatever, to fill it up. We throw in stones, earth, sand, anything, and smooth it over just enough for the trucks to pass. Around sixty yards along we hit another trench and have to do the same thing. Just before we reach the village we encounter a third one. The armored car can't get past it if we don't fill it in, but it's almost light so there's no time.

"I thought you were going to warn the villagers," I say to Simon.

"We are," he says. "From here. We'll put on the loud-speaker from here."

"They won't hear that!" I object. "And the sun is coming up. You can't attack in broad daylight. We never do!"

"Shut up, Ruth. You aren't in command here," Simon says. "You're an observer. Observe."

Just then a bullet hits the armored car in front of us and a cry goes up in Arabic from the village. Even I understand what they are shouting. "The Jews are here, the Jews are here!"

Gunfire erupts from the houses just ahead of us. Everyone crouches behind the armored car.

"So much for the element of surprise," Yaacov mutters. He turns on the loudspeaker, and one of his men begins to shout the message in Arabic, to leave and that no harm will come to them—but I'm sure no one in the village can hear it.

This is not starting out well.

CHAPTER 13

Apparently, there are around one hundred fighters. Thirty-five or so are in our group, the rest are coming in two groups from the north and the south. The village has around five hundred people.

A young Irgun fighter they call Yigael is shot as he moves from behind the armored car. He dies on the spot. The others seem horrified and, for the moment, are paralyzed. Then Yaacov motions them to follow him and they scramble toward the buildings, flattening themselves against the stone walls.

"Who's with me?" he calls.

"I am," Simon calls back.

"And me," says another. The three of them begin to attack the front houses.

Yaacov obviously has no idea how to direct his team. They are just running ahead and firing at random; no plan, nothing.

I brave the gunfire and run in a zigzag motion until I reach Yaacov.

"Now look," I say to him, panting, barely able to catch my breath. "You can't take the village this way. Tell your men to retreat."

"We aren't going to retreat," Yaacov says. "Have you seen the babies shot in their carriages by snipers in Jerusalem? Have you seen—"

"Oh, shut up!" I explode. "I've seen just as much as you have."

"'If a thief be found breaking up, and be smitten that he die, there shall no blood be shed for him.' Exodus 22:2," says Yaacov.

I speak to Simon. "Yaacov is spouting nonsense, and you're getting nowhere here."

Simon stares at me, then at Yaacov.

"Simon," Yaacov says, "harden your heart. These are the same people who murdered Yigael just minutes ago. These are the allies of Hitler. We are going to take the village and prove our worth."

"You can't prove anything this way!" I exclaim.

Simon seems to make a decision. "If you can't take it, Ruth," says Simon, "leave. We have a job to do."

Yaacov slaps him on the back. "Let's go."

There are snipers firing from the houses around us and from houses on higher ground, so nowhere is really safe. I slip in between two houses against a wall, gun at the ready should I need it. The fighting and shooting is fierce. Time seems to slow down.

I check the watch Aunt Sophie gave me. Two hours and they've just now taken the front row of houses. The groups finally meet up with each other and realize what difficulty they are in. I don't think they have captured more than twenty percent of the village after all that fighting.

"Look," I say to Yaacov, "there's a Palmach unit not far from here. Send a runner. Maybe they'll give you some help."

Much to my surprise, Yaacov agrees. "It can't hurt," he says.

Simon looks pale, like all the blood has been drained out of him. Many of the fighters are wounded; so far, two are dead. That's more than they are used to, and they all seem inflamed, furious with the villagers for putting up such a fight, for putting them in danger.

"Did you expect them to cooperate?" I ask.

"We're almost out of ammunition," Yaacov complains. "And we've made barely a dent in these snipers. Simon, I'm sending you back to headquarters. You bring me back all the TNT you can find. We'll fight the way we're used to fighting! The rest of you, hunt for ammunition in the houses we've taken. Go!"

Simon hurries off and the rest split up looking for ammunition. A small group continues to engage the Arabs, returning their fire. I hunker down in an alley and try to stay out of the way—I'm under strict orders from Aunt Sophie not to *do* anything.

Simon returns with the dynamite, which is quickly divided into countless small parcels. Yaacov orders everyone to follow him. One fighter runs up to a house and either throws the dynamite through the window or leaves it on the doorstep as the others cover him. When one house is destroyed, they go on to the next.

I try to stop them, telling them that they don't have to destroy the village house by house. In fact, it seems that there may be only a small group of Arab men who are actually armed. They have to concentrate on them. But they won't listen.

And then, suddenly, there is an entire Palmach section, and with the aid of a machine gun they secure the village. The snipers surrender without another casualty.

I find Simon. "You see," I say, "that's how it's done. You don't blow up houses with women and children in them if there is any other alternative."

"We didn't have a machine gun, though, did we?" he asks, exhausted. "We did our best."

"I know you think you did," I say, "but you need to be able to work in groups, to know which houses to take first. You need a plan. I'd better go talk to the Palmach commander."

The Palmach leader tells me that he has no intention of staying. He assumes that Yaacov and his men will occupy the village as ordered by the Haganah.

He takes his section, exhausted from fighting somewhere else all night, and leaves.

Suddenly Yaacov runs up to us. "Simon! Follow me! Mayer and David have gone crazy. They discovered Emmanuel dead in an alley, and they're out for revenge. They're just shooting anyone they can find! We have to stop them!"

Jews shooting unarmed Arabs? It can't be.

I run after them. We hear crying from inside a small hut. We look in. A young girl, face all smeared with blood, is curled over her mother. A little body lies under the mother's arm. I lift her arm. A baby boy. Both are dead.

My eyes meet Simon's. He turns to Yaacov. He tries to speak but words won't come out. I know what he's remembering. The ghetto, the Nazis, shooting at will, at mothers and children.

"No," he says.

"Come on," I say, grabbing his arm. "We have to find them!"

But we are always just behind them. We can't seem to catch up to them in the twisted streets. We try to follow the screams but the two of them must be running every which way.

Finally, we see them.

"Stop!" Yaacov shouts. They turn and glare at us, their eyes wild, full of hatred and revenge.

"Don't try to stop us!" David screams. "No more killing Jews! No more gas! No more! It ends here. We end it all here!"

Before Simon can stop me, I place myself in front of the door and raise my gun.

"Get out of the way," Mayer shrieks.

I don't say anything. They are beyond reason. But I won't let this happen. I point my gun at them.

David pulls the bolt on his gun.

Simon throws himself in front of me.

"For God's sake! She's my sister! She's all I've got left!"

That appears to get through to them. They pause. And then, slowly, they seem to come back to themselves, as if returning from a dream state. Finally, they lower their guns.

"Go help the others, make sure the village is secure," Yaacov says quietly.

They turn and leave.

I stare at Yaacov. "You're letting them back in action? Are you insane?"

"It's over," he says.

"Not for them," I say, gesturing at the carnage in the houses behind us.

Yaacov just shakes his head and walks away.

I slump against the door of the house. Simon does the same, beside me. But suddenly he raises his rifle. Aims. I look to see what he's aiming at. An Arab on a roof is pointing a gun straight at my head. Simon fires. So does the other. I throw myself to the ground. The bullet misses me. I look up. The Arab has fallen into the street beside me. Simon just saved my life.

I lie on the ground. All I can feel is blackness all around us. All I can hear are cries of fear and death.

"You should have let him shoot me," I say to Simon, looking up at him. "I'd rather be dead than have lived to see this."

And I crawl away from him and away from the screams and make my way back out onto the road. I grab a jeep, put it in gear, and screech away.

CHAPTER 14

I sit in Aunt Sophie's dining room and finish writing out my report. I don't write very well—I'm embarrassed about it, in fact. After all, I was ten when I stopped going to school, when the war started, and even though I've had some school since I got here, it's all been in Hebrew. So in a way, it's like I'm still at a grade school level with my writing. But Aunt Sophie has insisted that I write something.

I've told Aunt Sophie everything I saw. She was disgusted. She says the Haganah is going to issue a public statement saying that they have had nothing to do with what happened. She also tells me that the Arabs who were taken prisoner have been rounded up by some of the Irgun and Lehi fighters and paraded through the streets of Jerusalem, then dumped on Bab el Damesek. That's the road that runs north from Damascus Gate. Around two hundred and fifty people. The Arabs are saying that over one hundred villagers were killed, many women and children.

I don't cry as I repeat what I saw. I feel like a stone inside, cold and hard. And angry. Angry at Simon, and at the Nazis and the British and the Arabs and at everyone who hates us and makes us fight, turning some of us into monsters. The way that Yaacov spouted the Bible as an excuse, a *reason* to do anything, even kill. What is the First Commandment? Thou Shalt Not Kill. How can anyone think that this is what God wants?

And yet I kill. I think of the sixteen dead, all at my own hands. And the others. Should I have become a nurse or a medic? Someone who never carries a gun? Am I any different from Simon?

I excuse myself from the house and go sit beside Sima's

grave. I need to think. I don't understand anything.

If none of us fought, well, then the Arabs would just have slaughtered us. That's certainly what the Mufti promised. After all, we *never* asked for this. So when is it right to fight and when isn't it? The Haganah has always said that they will fight to defend themselves. That seems fair. But we are also on the offense even if we're only attacking villages that declare themselves enemies. The Irgun and Lehi, they will attack any Arab, any Englishman. But they say, just leave us alone and no one will be attacked. We're only fighting back.

I think of Sima, who never killed anyone.

"Tell me the answers, Sima," I say aloud. "You must know everything now." I pause. "Sima, I can't go back to Poland. I can't let them throw us out of here. And I can't just sit and not fight like we did in Poland. I can't. I can't!"

"Ruthie, dear, wake up. Wake up."

It's Aunt Sophie shaking me. I must've fallen asleep on Sima's grave. It's night, and I find I'm shivering.

"Come in, dear. Have some dinner. We have bread, and even some noodles!"

I follow her inside and sit down to a cozy dinner with her, Jonathan, Mika, and the baby, Hani-el. It's hard to imagine that what I saw yesterday could be as real as this. I find it hard to eat. I feel disoriented, as if I'm not sure anymore what's real and what's not.

Aunt Sophie puts me to bed in a spare room and tells me that she's placing me on nonfighting duty for a few days. Large convoys are reaching Jerusalem now and they need to be unloaded. Two hundred and fifty to three hundred trucks carry a lot of supplies.

I get up at sunrise and spend the day moving boxes. I like the work. It's hard but you don't have to think, or worry about your section and how to keep them alive or how to keep yourself alive. In a way, it's relaxing. After three days of it I almost feel like I've been on holiday.

It's my fourth day and I am moving boxes that have been unloaded into trucks and cars for transport around the city when someone yells, "The convoy. The Hadassah Convoy. It's under attack!"

No, I say to myself, it can't be. Only this morning Aunt Sophie had checked with the British officer in charge of the road up to the Hebrew University and the Hadassah Hospital on Mount Scopus. The road always used to be under threat and under attack by the Arabs but finally, at the beginning of April, the British took over a building that overlooked it and the Arabs had not attacked once since then. Aunt Sophie even double-checked with the British officer this morning, because eighty people were to go on those buses—the top doctors and nurses from the hospital, the most esteemed professors from the university.

I drop my boxes and race up the stairs in the warehouse we're using, then up the stairs through the trapdoor to the roof. There are already a number of people on the roof and we can quite clearly see the convoy under fire in the distance. We can also see the British standing there, looking on, doing nothing.

Someone has binoculars. I borrow them to get a closer look. A roadblock has been set up, and the first car can't get past it. As I watch I see a grenade hit the first car. The people in the car run out. Two are on fire. The others are shot as they run. None of us can move. We are glued to the spot, watching. All day it goes on. According to people here who run in and out with news, the British won't let the Haganah near. One officer apparently said that "perhaps this is a good reply to Deir Yassin." I can't leave the roof. I can't stop watching. It takes all day as one by one the people in the cars run out of bullets and the Arabs kill them, car by car. I feel so helpless. So furious.

Finally as night comes I make my way back to

Aunt Sophie's. And there, for the first time, I see her cry.

"I sent them," she says. "I knew so many of them! So many dear friends. So many husbands and wives, fathers, mothers—slaughtered. And the British standing by doing nothing! And our best doctors, how badly we need them . . ." She is completely distraught.

I make her some hot tea and find a little brandy to put in it. I make her drink it. She wipes her eyes.

"It's *not* the same as Deir Yassin," she says. "Because if we had known in time, we would have stopped what happened there. You *did* stop it. The British knew and did nothing. And not for the first time," she says bitterly. "I could tell you so many times when they have stood by, or actually helped the Arabs. Do you know who drove the truck that blew up Ben Yehudah Street?"

I shake my head.

"Two British soldiers, that's who. I don't know how I'll be able to deal with the British from now on. Six more weeks until they leave. Can't come soon enough."

"Aunt Sophie, please send me back to my section," I say.

"Are you ready?"

"Yes," I answer. And suddenly I know I am. "Standing there, feeling so helpless today, it made me see that I need to be able to do something. What happened in Deir Yassin isn't us. It isn't me. Even most of those Irgun fighters weren't being vicious on purpose. They just didn't know a better way to fight, the right way."

Aunt Sophie shakes her head.

"I'm not making excuses for them. Not at all. But I know it isn't our way and I want to go back and fight. I'm not going to stand by and watch my people be slaughtered. Never again."

"I can get you on the convoy leaving tomorrow morning," Aunt Sophie says briskly. "Your section is still fighting around Ramle, trying to take the villages around there. Come here."

I go over to her and she gives me a big hug.

"They'd want us to survive," she says softly. "In spite of everything, they'd want us to survive."

Then she lets me go.

I nod and turn away. By *they*, she means Mother and Father and my sister Hannah and my brother Joshua and her husband Zev and our grandparents and all our cousins and all our friends and everyone, dead at the hands of the Nazis.

"You know that we've had a number of reports of Germans fighting alongside the Arabs?" she says.

"Really?" I say, my stomach twisting just at the thought.

"Oh, yes. And Poles and even Italians. Nazis who weren't caught, and came here to finish what they started."

"If I ran across one of them when I was fighting, I don't know what I'd do," I say.

"You'd keep your head and think of your section," Aunt Sophie says. "And fight twice as hard."

Were we all cursed by God to be put on the earth at this time?

MAY 1948

CHAPTER 15

I walk down the hall to the nurses' station. "Excuse me," I say to a young woman sitting behind the desk, "could you tell me where Zvi Bernstein is?"

"Are you a relative?" she asks.

"He has no relatives," I answer. "I'm his, uh . . ." I don't know what to say. Fiancée? But we aren't officially engaged.

"A close friend?" she suggests, smiling warmly.

"Yes," I answer, thankful she's helped me out.

"I'm glad you're here," she says.

"Well," I say, "I would have been here sooner but I couldn't get away from my section."

"I understand, of course," she says. "It's just that he won't talk to any of us. He's had three operations on his legs, you know."

"And?" I ask, hardly daring to hear her answer.

"And the doctor thinks he'll walk again, but only if he wants to make the effort *now*. Otherwise, his muscles will all deteriorate."

"I don't understand," I say. "Maybe there are two Zvis here on this ward. My Zvi is always telling jokes, always laughing. . . ."

"Zvi Bernstein? He hasn't said a word in three weeks. Only 'yes' or 'no' to the doctor's questions."

"May I see him?" I ask.

"Come with me." She motions me to follow her. As we walk down the corridor I flash back to the moment Zvi got hurt. We were retreating across a field, and he was just in front of me. Suddenly a huge explosion and Zvi is down, both legs a mass of blood. He'd stepped on a mine, and his legs were full of shrapnel. I couldn't carry him alone, so Karl ran over but he stepped on a mine and was killed instantly. Then Fanny ran up, threw Zvi over her shoulder, and got him out.

The nurse leads me into the ward. There are eight beds, four along each wall. She walks me over to the third bed. Zvi is lying with his eyes open, staring at the ceiling.

"Zvi!" I exclaim. I rush to him and bend over, kissing his cheek. He doesn't respond. He doesn't move a muscle.

"Zvi! It's me. What is it? What's the matter?"

Something is *very* wrong. I look at the nurse. She shrugs. "Maybe he'll cheer up now that you're here."

She finds me a chair, and I sit down beside him.

"Zvi, don't be mad at me," I say. "I couldn't get away. The fighting has been so bad and Nate just couldn't spare me but I told him today that I was coming here, with or without his permission, so he said 'yes.' Zvi, look at me!"

He just stares into nothing.

"Zvi, today's the day! Ben-Gurion is going to declare the State of Israel. Right here in Tel Aviv."

He closes his eyes and turns his head away from me. I decide to try another tack.

"Okay, Zvi, Joe told me that this joke is just for you. God allows Moses to choose whatever promised land he wants. Moses thinks hard and finally decides. The only trouble is, Moses has a stutter. So he wants to answer 'California' but it comes out 'Ca-Ca-' and God says, 'Canaan, that wasteland? Well, if it's what you want, it's what you'll get!'"

Zvi doesn't even respond.

"Joe is going to be very disappointed that his joke didn't even warrant a smile," I chide Zvi.

Nothing. He still hasn't said a word to me.

"You know that we've taken Safed," I say to him. "Two thousand Jews in Safed, twelve thousand Arabs. The British turned over the police station, the Teggart fort, the Citadel, everything to the Arabs, figuring they would certainly win the town easily. The Jews there, who are all religious, old, many of them mystics, they didn't run away. The British offered to evacuate all the Jews but they refused. In Tiberias when the British offered to evacuate the Arabs they accepted. See, that's the difference. Twelve thousand to two thousand, but they wouldn't leave. Our section was snuck in there, Zvi; it was amazing. They treated us so well—the Rabbis even ordered everyone to work building trenches on Pesach.

"And you know, the Jews of Safed were great friends with the Arabs. One day I was in a trench with a Jewish tailor called Shmuel. He and his Arab friend were shouting to each other. Shmuel called, 'Assad, go home, your wife will be worrying.' And then Shmuel tried to shoot his gun but it jammed, so Assad called to him, 'And your wife, she won't worry also? And don't try to shoot your gun when it's cold; it won't work!' Then they started shooting at each other! Every move we made the Arabs knew about it immediately because some friend would tell them. A group of Irgun men arrived there, too, and agreed to take orders from Haganah. Simon was one of them, Zvi. I was really proud of him."

I'm waiting for Zvi to react, just a little.

"The Arabs evacuated," I say, "but we lost a lot—well—never mind." I suddenly realize Zvi doesn't need to hear about any more deaths.

I won't tell him that we lost all the kibbutzim in the Etzion block, and that when the kibbutzniks of Kfar Etzion surrendered they were gathered in the square and massacred. One hundred and fifty people killed; only four somehow survived.

"And you know Jaffa is ours now?" I say. "And the Irgun seems to have helped, by shelling it, or at least that's what I heard. . . ."

I want to tell him that tomorrow we may *really* be at

war, surrounded by hostile armies all ready to invade, that he has to stop this silly behavior, that he has to get better, but finally, I just sit and hold his hand.

"Zvi," I say, "you have to get better. I need you. Zvi, look at me!"

But he won't look at me. His eyes are closed and he looks away. What is he thinking? What is wrong?

I sit with him quietly all day, until around five. Then I go outside for a little break. The streets are filled with people dancing, laughing, hugging each other. I let myself be pulled into the hora. We are a state! The moment Zvi had always dreamed of. I dance for him and for Karl and for Sima and for myself, twirling round and round, singing at the top of my lungs, feeling almost happy for a brief moment.

I notice that people are working on top of the hospital, and I'm told that they are painting a red cross on it so when the city is attacked tomorrow the Arabs won't bomb the hospital.

I go back up to Zvi, who is lying just as I left him. "Zvi," I say, "it's your dream. Everyone is out dancing. We have a home now! Zvi, you have to get better. You *will* get better. The doctors say your legs will be fine. Zvi. Look at me!"

But he won't look. He won't talk. He won't budge.

I fall asleep in the chair beside him and am woken by the sound of planes and huge explosions all around us. We're under attack! Now it is not just the Arabs in Palestine we have to fight. All the Arab states surrounding us will try to wipe us off the map.

The hospital is being targeted. Everyone who can leave by themselves does so, but Zvi needs help. The young man in the bed next to Zvi's is running out. He has a cast on one arm.

"Please help me carry Zvi down," I call to him.

The fellow stops, comes back, puts his good arm around

Zvi on one side. I take Zvi's other arm. He is limp like a doll.

"Zvi," I scold, "we are *not* leaving without you. If you don't try to move, to walk, probably this nice young boy—what's your name?—"

"Ben."

"Ben will die, and so will I. So are you going to help us or not?"

At that Zvi actually looks at me. His eyes have no expression. He says, "Just leave me."

"We're not leaving you," I say. "Now walk."

"Leave me," he repeats.

"No."

"I said leave me!" he screams, and I've *never* heard him sound like that: angry. So angry it scares me.

I stand my ground, though.

"No!" I shout back at him. "We won't leave you!"

"God damn you," he screams, but he rests his arms on our shoulders and tries to move his legs. They don't move well—all we need is for him not to be a dead weight.

When we get outside we head for the ditches around the hospital. I look up. The Arab Spitfires are flying so low I can see the faces of the pilots. They're laughing!

We try to run but we are too slow, holding Zvi. Ben screams and his legs fold under him. We're almost at the ditch. I drag Zvi in first, then go back for Ben. As I'm pulling Ben in, suddenly I am hit. It feels like my shoulder is coming off.

Zvi doesn't notice. He's babbling. Crying.

"They took all my family. Everyone naked. Have you ever seen your parents naked? They were so humiliated. They lined us up over the ditch.

"GET ME OUT OF THIS PIT."

"GET ME OUT!"

He's shrieking. "And you had to face the ditch and they

shot you from behind and Mama pulled me in front of her at the last minute and she pushed me into the pit, and I landed on my sister! On my dead sister! And then Mama fell on top of me. But she wasn't quite dead yet. No. She screamed. She moaned. Forever.

"GET THE BODIES OFF ME!

"GET ME OUT OF HERE!"

I grab Zvi with my good arm and pull him to me. The other arm is starting to go numb.

"Zvi, it's me. It's Ruth. Your Ruth. Zvi, can you hear me? Can you *hear* me?"

"Ruth?"

"Yes, it's Ruth. Zvi, you never cried for them. Zvi, you've been telling jokes and fighting. Zvi, for God's sakes, cry for them!"

"I can't, Ruth!"

But then he lets out a scream that is so terrible, a scream full of all the anguish, the fear, and suffering, a scream so dreadful I feel that the entire world must stand still to hear it. To witness it.

I am crying, my arms wrapped around him, his head on my good shoulder, the other one quite numb now and I feel him gasp for air, like he can't breathe, and then I start to feel very light-headed and then I realize that he's crying, and I say, "Zvi, I love you, Zvi."

"Ruth. Ruthie? What is it?" His voice comes to me from far away. "Oh my God. She's been hit. Ruth, Ruthie! Stay awake. You're going into shock. Ruth! Stay with me! We need help here!"

"I've been shot, too!" I hear Ben's voice. He sounds a bit indignant at being ignored. That strikes me as funny.

"Zvi. Ben's been shot, too! Don't ignore him, Zvi. Ben's been shot, too." And I giggle.

"Thatagirl. No, I won't forget about him. It's just a flesh wound. He'll be all right."

Zvi is screaming for help, and then I feel myself being lifted and then—

When I wake up everything is dark. I wonder if I'm dead. If I am I have a few things I'd like to discuss with the all-powerful one. Quite a few things.

"Hello?" I call in Yiddish, forgetting to speak Hebrew.

"Ruth?" It is Zvi.

"Where are you?"

"In the bed beside you."

"Are we dead?"

"Not yet."

"Everything hurts," I whisper.

"You took a bullet in the shoulder, but you'll be fine," he says.

"How are you?"

There is a pause.

"I think I'm going to be all right."

"Good," I say. And I close my eyes.

For no reason, a prayer my mother used to say suddenly pops into my head. Until this moment I'd forgotten it completely.

Baruch ata Adonai Eloheinu, melech haolom, shehecheyano vekiyemanu hehigainu lazeman hazeh.

Blessed is the Lord our God, Ruler of the Universe, for giving us life, for sustaining us, and for enabling us to reach this joyous day.

Karl is dead. Sima is dead. Before the war is over, who knows which of us will die. I still don't know how I feel about God. But I think I'm starting to understand why my mother loved that prayer. Because, despite everything, I'm happy just to be here.

"Ruth?"

"Yes?"

"When the war is over, and we're back at Kibbutz David, will you meet me in your garden? After dark?"

"Yes, Zvi." I smile. "I will."

And I think to myself that even if I get back to Kibbutz David, and the garden has been blasted away by the Arab attack, well, I'll just plant it again, and again, and again, and I'll replant it a hundred times if I have to but I will *never* give it up, I will *never* leave it. Because it's home. Because as of today, I have a home.

AFTERWORD

In 1917, Britain, the Mandatory Power in charge of Palestine, promised its support for a Jewish state in Palestine with the Balfour Declaration. Jews all over the world were thrilled to hear that finally they might have a homeland. But Arab riots and Arab force proved to be an effective way to make the British back away from their promise. Arab riots in Palestine in 1921, 1929, and 1936–39 resulted in the British turning away from their promise and restricting Jewish immigration. This was a terrible tragedy, because even as Hitler began to wipe out the Jewish population of Europe, which ended with the death of six million Jews, Britain refused to open up the country to immigration. An illegal network was formed, and during and after the war almost 70,000 Jews were smuggled into Palestine.

After the war, the United Nations sent a delegation to Palestine, and in 1947, it recommended partition of the land into an Arab state and a Jewish state, with Jerusalem as an international site. Even though the territory awarded by the UN to the Jewish population (around 650,000 then) was only one-eighth of the original land promised in 1917, the Jews were ecstatic. On November 29, the United Nations held its vote. The partition resolution passed thirty-three to thirteen, with ten abstentions—one of them being Britain.

The next day, November 30, a Jewish bus traveling from Netanya to Jerusalem was attacked. Five people were killed, seven wounded. It seems that the Arab leadership hoped to win by force what they had lost in the vote at the United Nations.

This is the story of the undeclared, or unofficial war. Some names are real, others are not. There wasn't a real Kibbutz David just off the road from Tel Aviv to Jerusalem. There really was a terrible episode at Deir Yassin—although I have read at least ten different versions of it, and there seems to be little agreement on what really happened. The number of Arabs killed that I use is an Arab estimate. The Jewish estimate is actually higher.

Survivors of the Holocaust made up a large number of the fighting forces of the Haganah. Survivors did not hesitate to volunteer. They felt they had nothing to lose, but they had a country to gain.

GLOSSARY

Arab Liberation Army: Ostensibly a volunteer force of Arab army veterans, in reality it was a group of mercenaries supported by Arab countries under the command of Fawzi al-Qawukii. At its height there were seven thousand men. Their purpose was to destabilize Palestine and take as much land as possible before the official State of Israel was declared and the official Arab armies attacked.

Auschwitz: A complex that included a concentration camp, an extermination camp, and a labor camp, established April 27, 1940, and situated in Galicia, near the border of Upper Silesia.

Balagan: Hebrew for chaos, a big mess.

Begin, Menachem: Leader of Irgun Zvai Leumi.

Ben-Gurion, David: Chairman of the Jewish Agency during World War II, head of the unofficial government in Palestine, he became the first prime minister of the State of Israel.

Bren gun: Fast, light machine guns made in Czechoslovakia.

Eretz Israel: Hebrew name for the land of Israel. Also the official Hebrew designation of the area governed by British mandate from the end of World War II until 1948.

Gadna: Paramilitary youth organization, training 13- to 18-year-olds.

Haganah: The Haganah was founded by the Jewish population in Palestine in 1920 as a clandestine self-defense organization. Haganah literally means "defense," and between 1945 and 1948 it was a purely defensive force. However, this eventually became impossible. In 1948, with the declaration of the State of Israel, the Haganah became the Israel Defense Forces, or Zahal.

Irgun: Irgun Zvai Leumi consisted of around two thousand members in 1947. Headed by Menachem Begin, they attacked the British in a kind of guerrilla warfare and were considered terrorists by the British and by the Haganah. Also known as *Etzel,* an abbreviation of Irgun Zvai Leumi.

Kibbutz: A kibbutz is a large cooperative settlement. People share work, property, and the fruits of their labor equally. The children usually live together and are educated and looked after communally.

Palestine: The Old Testament refers to this land, on the eastern shore of the Mediterranean, as Canaan. In 1920 it became a British mandate. The British left on May 14, 1948.

Palmach: Elite, crack troops of the Haganah, founded in 1941. Its members were incorporated into the Israel Defense Forces in 1948.

Partition: On November 29, 1947, the UN General Assembly at Lake Success, New York, passed a resolution recommending the partition of Palestine between Jews and Arabs. The vote was thirty-three to thirteen. Ten countries abstained, including Britain.

Passover: "Pesach" in Hebrew. A Jewish holiday that lasts for eight days, in which the exodus of the Jewish people and their release from slavery is remembered.

Sabra: A person born in Israel.

Sapper: An explosives expert.

Shabbat: Beginning sundown on Friday and ending sundown on Saturday, the Jewish Sabbath.

Sten gun: Small, light, British-made submachine gun.

Stern gang: Lohamei Herut Israel, or fighters for the freedom of Israel. Also known as LHI, or Lehi, acronym of the name. An even more militant group of fighters than the Irgun, their members numbered around four hundred in 1947. Also regarded as terrorists by the British and by the Haganah.

Sukkot: The harvest festival, or the Festival of Booths. It recalls the experience of the Jewish people when they were wandering in the desert. A sukkah, a crude hut made of wood, is built outdoors, and families eat and sometimes sleep in it.